COLD
WAR

ALSO BY BRADLEY WRIGHT

Alexander King

THE SECRET WEAPON

COLD WAR

MOST WANTED

Alexander King Prequels

WHISKEY & ROSES

VANQUISH

KING'S RANSOM

KING'S REIGN

SCOURGE

Lawson Raines

WHEN THE MAN COMES AROUND

SHOOTING STAR

Saint Nick

SAINT NICK

SAINT NICK 2

COLD WAR

Bradley Wright/King's Ransom Publishing

www.bradleywrightauthor.com

COLD WAR/ Bradley Wright. -- 1st ed.

ISBN - 978-0-9973926-8-5

For Team X
The best advanced reader team on the planet. Everything you do
for my work is highly valuable, but what you do for me as a
friend is priceless.

"If the world is cold, make it your business to build fires."

— HORACE TRAUBEL

In the field of biological weapons, there is almost no prospect of detecting a pathogen until it has been used in an attack.

— BARTON GELLMAN

COLD
WAR

1

WASHINGTON, DC

"THEY'RE ALL INFECTED."

"What?"

President of the United States, Bobby Gibbons, stared at his secretary of health and human services, Andrew Richards, like he had two heads.

The president continued. "Just yesterday you said only half of the town had become ill."

"It's not happening as fast in Yupak as the other town, but it's a terrible situation."

Two weeks ago, and the day after President Gibbons was sworn in, officials brought him into his office and told him that a small town in Alaska had all died from some fast-moving, ultracontagious virus. Just over a hundred people were dead within a week. Something completely unheard of, and alarm bells had gone off that this wasn't just some fluke. Everyone in Gibbons's cabinet thought it smelled of biowarfare. Or at least the beginnings of it. The reason it was even more of a red flag than usual was because Dmitry Kuznetsov, a world-renowned Russian biochemist and virologist, flew into Seattle from Moscow several months ago for a World Health Conference . . . and he never left. Now that the people in another town, not far from the one that had been wiped out, had all fallen ill as well, there was almost zero doubt left that something was amiss. And President Gibbons was happy he'd already made the decision to send in an agent to try to dig in to where they thought the problem could be brewing.

"Somebody is testing a virus," CIA Director Robert Lucas said with confidence. "I can feel it."

"All right, Robert," the president said. "We can get into that in a minute." The president shifted his focus to the secretary of health. "Right now, I want to hear from who you brought with you, Andrew."

Andrew cleared his throat. "Of course, Mr. President, this is Donna Ingram. She's been a top virologist for years. I've given her all the data, as you asked."

The president reached across the couch in the Oval Office and shook Donna's hand. Next to the tall and big-shouldered Andrew, Donna looked even more petite. Her short dark hair bobbed as the president shook her tiny hand. She seemed young, but the president could never tell anymore. When you get above sixty, everyone seems young.

"Thank you for coming on such short notice, Ms. Ingram. Give it to me straight. We need to know what engines to fire next to get ahead of this thing."

"Thanks for having me. I won't waste your time. This is absolutely a manufactured virus. But that isn't what scares me."

The president sat back in his seat. "Well, it is what scares me, so now I'm really nervous."

"You should be," Donna said.

She produced a folder and took a sheet of paper out. She extended it toward the president. He took it, but it all looked like a foreign language to him. "Just explain it to me."

"Chart one shows the incubation period from the town that was completely wiped out. As you can see, there was little to none. It just wiped people out. Chart two, fresh data from my biologist who was sent in to Yupak yesterday shows that the last few people to get sick had been in contact with the first people to get it over a week ago. Only just showing signs of being sick this morning."

"Isn't that a good thing?" the president said.

"It's much worse," Robert chimed in. "If this really is a manufactured virus, whoever is creating it will want a long incubation period."

"That's right," Donna said. "If someone is wanting to infect a massive amount of people, they are going to want the symptoms to lie dormant for as long as possible."

The president understood now why it was bad. "So those who are infected will go on about their lives not knowing they have it, meanwhile infecting a much larger amount of people."

"Exactly," Donna said. "It seems to me that they unleashed two different strands of this at the same time. One to Eleanor, Alaska, where the town died off in a week, and the other to Yupak where only two have died in probably two weeks, but still everyone is sick. They've already learned a lot about their virus, just in this one test. I'm afraid it's time to clear out that region of Alaska, Mr. President. There could already be another testing strain in another town, and we don't even know it."

President Gibbons stood. "Thank you, Andrew, and thank you, Ms. Ingram, for coming. Please continue to update me by the half hour. We'll take it from here."

Donna shook his hand and stopped as she walked toward the door. "Mr. President, call me Donna. And if I may?"

"Of course."

"If this is what we all think it is, if this makes it to the lower forty-eight states, this could be *the one* we've all been fearing. It could bring all of North America down."

2

UTQIAGVIK (BARROW), ALASKA

ALEXANDER KING BEGAN his walk to the only bar in town. Everything was frozen. Not in a hypothetical sense but literally: all things outside were frozen solid. And had been for months. When King met with the president of the United States two weeks ago, and he'd asked King to take the most important assignment of his career, even though President Gibbons told him it was Alaska, King had no idea it would be like this.

Pure misery.

The ice crunched beneath his feet as he walked the snow-covered dirt road. There was no pavement in Barrow. The weather would never allow for any such thing. All the roads had to consist of gravel and dirt. The road he walked along was just that under the four inches of frozen snow he plodded through. On both sides of the road were rows of wooden houses. All just like the one he was staying in. His one-bedroom, four-room house was as basic as it gets. While he thought he would never long for the small flat he'd stayed in for months in London almost a year ago, he did. And he certainly never imagined he'd long for the weather. But London now seemed like a tropical paradise.

Not only had the average temperature been negative five degrees Fahrenheit, but until a week ago, there had also been no sun. Zero. He supposed he felt fortunate that his assignment hadn't started until Barrow's sixty-five days of night were over, but today had exactly two hours of sun. That's it. Oh, and a couple of hours of what they called *civil twilight,* which basically meant you could walk the streets without tripping over something in front of you. It was like a lamp on in the other room in your house. You could see, just not very well.

King wrapped his scarf a little tighter around his neck. He was thankful that it wasn't as windy that night as it had been the previous six days. This was the third night in a row he'd made this walk after his day sleep due to his night shift at the Volkov Mining Company. Normally he would never leave the house if he didn't have to in weather like this, but the weather and the days filled with night weren't even the worst part about Barrow. The worst part was that you couldn't buy liquor without a city-issued permit. Which meant no permit for an undercover special agent like King. He obviously wouldn't be going to the police station to obtain that permit under any circumstance, because he had to keep his head down and do his work. He also prayed to the gods that he wouldn't be there in Frozen Land long enough to really need it.

In a sense, he was lucky to be able to make this walk at all. Only three months ago, there was no such thing as a bar at all in Barrow. The village voted that there could be only one, as they thought it would help keep people from buying their booze from bootleggers. King honestly felt like he'd stepped back in time, or into another world entirely. Most people in the town of four thousand were native Alaskans. A lot of them still only spoke Iñupiaq, the language they'd known their entire lives. King sensed how out of place he was. Only a small percentage of people looked like King, and an even smaller amount differed from there. The uptick in the Caucasian population had been the recent influx of Russians moving in. Something it didn't take long for King to figure out that wasn't a popular thing here in the village.

So here he was, in the northernmost city in the United States, the ninth most northern city in the world, walking to a bar like he would in any other city at nine o'clock at night if he'd run out of booze. Some things never change.

It was quiet in the frozen town. No one was really out on the roads. The frozen arctic ocean just a couple hundred feet away ensured not much else could make noise either. Since it wasn't time for one of the two commercial flights a day, the airport was silent as well. The fact that there were no roads in and out of this region of Alaska—not to mention no boats could float on ice—the term isolation had been taken to a whole other level. But right in front of him sat the most bustling place in all of Barrow—and for King, the only piece of his home he could get so far from the lower forty-eight: good ole Kentucky bourbon. And thankfully, a heater.

King walked through the door and into the warmth. His cheeks felt like needles were stabbing into them as the heat penetrated his cold skin. The bar wasn't big. Probably the size of a McDonald's in total, but decorated much differently. The hardwood floor met the hardwood walls, which held the likes of deer heads, moose busts, and even a full-sized Kodiac bear in the far corner. The bar top ran along the entire right side of the room, ending in the restrooms and a juke box, which fortunately was playing "Walk The Line" by Johnny Cash.

Though the population of Barrow was 65 percent native, the bar, at the moment, was nearly 100 percent Caucasian. King had heard some chatter over the last couple of days that alcohol was severely frowned upon by most natives. That was clear by the patrons gathered there. In the middle of all the four-top tables in the bar was a pool table. Probably the most popular place in the city since the bar had opened. Certainly one of the most dangerous as well. King had already seen two fights in two visits, and they were already ramping up, from what he could tell. The place was full. Only one lone seat at the far end of the bar. He put his head down and made his way there.

King didn't plan on staying long. His second security shift of the day started in just an hour. The first few days on the job he was just being trained on how to keep the Volkov Mining site secure.

Tonight he would start the real reason he was sent to the northern edge of the world: to try to stop the manufacturing, and therefore the spread, of a virus that could potentially put an end to the American way of life as everyone knew it.

3

KING REMOVED HIS SCARF AND HIS COAT AND DRAPED THEM on the back of his stool. As he removed his wool skull cap and ran his fingers through his thick brown hair, the other reason he'd made the freezing cold walk to the bar three nights in a row began walking his way.

And she was really something else.

Her sandy-brown hair bounced in her work ponytail. From the looks of her white V-neck T-shirt and snug blue jeans, it was clear she knew how to stay in shape. But it was her smile that melted what was left of the cold for King, and it was at full sparkle when she spoke to him.

"Let me guess. Bourbon, neat."

"Is there any other way?"

"Not sure, I'm a tequila girl. But judging by your accent, you come by your love of bourbon honestly."

She picked up one of only three bottles of bourbon the bar had—Maker's Mark—and poured him a drink. The other two bottles weren't up to par.

"Kentucky," King said.

"Yeah?" She set the glass down in front of him. "What's a Kentucky boy doin' all the way out here in the middle of nowhere?"

King took the glass in his hand and gave her a nod. "Thank you. And I just needed a change of scenery."

"Bullshit," she said with a grin. "People go to Cancun for a change of scenery, not Barrow freakin' Alaska."

"That right?" he said as he took a sip.

"That's right. People are either here because they were raised here, trying to strike it rich here . . ." She nodded to the Russians who were getting obnoxiously loud by the pool table. "Or they are running from something. Now I know you weren't born here, and I also know that you work security at Volkov Mining, so you aren't trying to get rich . . . so what was her name?"

"Natalie," King lied. Though that was her name, it wasn't why he was in Alaska. He was going to have to get used to lying, no matter how much he hated it. But at least there was a bit of truth to it.

She was drying a glass with her towel. "Well, she must have been something to drive you all the way out here."

A man approached the bar aggressively and slammed a beer mug down on the bar top. "Who the hell you talking to, Cali?"

Cali took a step back. "Excuse me? You can't talk to me like that, Ryker."

"Okay." The man shifted his focus to King. "Who the hell are you, and who do you think you're talking to? She's with me."

Ryker was a big man, young, probably late twenties. He was clearly native Iñupiat by his dark hair, accent, and other

Native American features. King didn't care who the man was; he only cared about not getting involved.

King held up his hands. "I don't want any trouble."

"Make no mistake," Cali said. "I am not with you, Ryker. Leave the man alone, he's new in town."

"I can see that. We don't take too kindly to newcomers around here."

"Really?" Cali interrupted again. "You're going to be *that* guy? Mister Cliché Townie?"

Ryker looked over and pointed his finger at Cali. "You shut your mouth."

King stood from his bar stool. He hadn't meant to. It was just a reflex. He could *not* afford to make an example out of this guy.

Ryker got in his face. His breath wreaked of alcohol. "Ooh, the big man stood up. You gonna do something?"

Cali rounded the corner of the bar and forced her way in between King and Ryker. She pushed Ryker back, but he grabbed her by the shoulder and tossed her aside. King watched as she fell to the floor, and before he could stop himself, King two-arm shoved Ryker so hard his feet left the ground and he landed hard on his back.

King instantly regretted it, because now he knew he was going to have to take a beating. He couldn't be the new guy in town who knew how to fight. King just hoped someone would pull Ryker off him before it got too bad.

As soon as Ryker got back to his feet, the door to the bar opened behind him. A man in a police coat walked in and momentarily drew the attention of the bar. Ryker didn't turn around. He was seething, solely focused on King.

"Ryker, no!" Cali shouted.

Ryker stepped forward and hit King in the forehead

about as hard as King had ever been hit. It had been near impossible to resist blocking the attack and countering like he was capable of doing, but he was just hoping for the police officer to hurry over. Ryker moved down to King and picked him up by his shirt. Cali grabbed at Ryker, but he used his free hand to pound King in the stomach. The air left him as he slumped back onto the floor.

"Sheriff, do something!" Cali shouted.

"You aren't so tough now, are you?" Ryker stood over him.

Thankfully the sheriff wrapped his arms around Ryker's chest and pulled him backward. "All right, that's enough!" he shouted. The sheriff moved Ryker aside and pulled King up. King was still trying to catch his breath. "You in here causing trouble, newcomer?"

"Ryker is the only one causing trouble, Josiah," Cali said to the sheriff.

Ryker stepped back up, but the sheriff held him back.

"You always let a woman fight for you?" Ryker was high on booze and adrenaline, and he wanted more.

"Get the hell out of here, Ryker," the sheriff said. "In fact, *everyone* get out!"

The jeers from the patrons were loud. They weren't happy about having their night ruined. Out of the corner of his eye he could see the Russians begin taking their frustrations out on guys who were clearly with Ryker.

The sheriff pulled his gun and turned to the angered men. "No more fights tonight, you hear me? Go home, or go to jail!" Then he turned back to Cali and King. "Damn Russians. You one of them, blue eyes?" he said to King.

"He's not Russian. He just got hired on for security at Volkov. He's from the States."

"Yeah?" The sheriff walked over. "You stir things up like this where you're from? 'Cause I won't have it here."

King wiped the blood from his mouth. "I told him I didn't want any trouble."

"Really? What I saw, you put him on his back. That's not easy. He's dumb, but he's strong."

"He was just trying to protect me," Cali said. "Ryker pushed me."

"He pushed you?" The sheriff's focus shifted. He was upset.

It was clear to King that Cali was a very popular woman in Barrow.

"It's fine, Josiah," Cali said. "He's drunk." Then to King. "I'm really sorry. Let me get you some ice."

"I'm fine."

"He hit you pretty hard," the sheriff said. "You sure you're all right?"

"I've had worse," King said.

If they only knew.

"I doubt it, Ryker's a boxer. Always did hit like a truck."

The sheriff tried to help King over to the bar stool, but King shrugged him off. "I'm fine. Thank you."

"Listen, I'm sorry I came at you like that." The sheriff adjusted the holster jutting out from his hip. "We don't get a lot of newcomers except these damn Russian guys. Didn't mean to lump you in. Welcome to Barrow. Name's Josiah.

"Xavier," King said. "Friends call me X." The name that his handler and longtime friend Sam Harrison had given him was one that felt familiar. People had been calling him Xander for years, X for short. The name Xavier made it more natural for him as a cover.

"Nice to meet you, X. Piece of advice?"

"Of course," King said.

"Keep your head down for a while till people get used to you. You're not off to a great start. You don't want to get on the bad side of guys like Ryker. All it is, is more trouble for you. Then that will be more trouble for me."

Cali handed King a bar towel full of ice. He pointed at Cali. "She always getting guys in trouble?"

Josiah laughed. "You bet. Ever since she moved here from Los Angeles, Cali's been constantly stirring the pot."

"I can't help that you all don't get many new women here. How you boys handle it is your fault, not mine."

Josiah clapped King on the shoulder. "Don't get any ideas. I've been trying for six years."

Josiah's shoulder radio squawked. *Josiah, we've got some trouble a street over from the bar. MORE fighting.*

"Shit, I'll see you all later." The sheriff walked away as he answered, "I'm right here, I'll handle it."

The bar was empty. Neil Young was singing about a harvest moon on the jukebox, but the rest of the room was quiet.

"Sorry about all this," Cali said as she wiped down the counter. "Not much of a welcome. These idiots are going to get this place shut down."

"I gather this establishment isn't popular in some circles here?"

"Barely got it open. I convinced people in a town hall meeting that it would cut down on the horrible bootlegging problem we have here."

"Is it working?"

"I think they are just recruiting customers here. The entire thing might have been a bad idea. I just wanted a little piece of home here. Guess I didn't think it through. Never wanted to make things worse."

King set down the ice and finished his drink. "Thanks for the ice. And the drink." He pulled out some cash.

Cali rushed over. "Oh no. Put your money away." She nodded to the cut on his forehead. "You already more than paid for it."

"Thank you."

"And don't feel bad. Ryker has worked over some of the toughest guys in Alaska. It wasn't a fair fight."

King almost laughed, but he kept it to himself and just gave her a smile as he wrapped his scarf around his neck.

"Okay then. Off to work. Have a nice night, Cali."

Cali gave him that smile that helped his decision to come back to the bar tomorrow. "Night, X. See you tomorrow."

4

King swiped his badge to clock in and walked over to the security desk. It had been a long time since he'd been in uniform and the first time wearing a cop-like security getup. Volkov Mining was a massive place. The wall of thirty camera monitors in front of him would have told him that, even if he'd never actually seen the rest of the site. The area consisted of a large building, which he was in, and then ten smaller wooden buildings constructed around it in a circle. If the site were a body, he was in the brain. Each of the small buildings had one security camera on the outside of them. The rest were scattered around the large building he was sitting in, watching hallways, as well as around parts of the outside.

During his training, he'd seen the inside of every building, except for one at the far end, the only one of the wooden buildings that was attached via a hallway to the building King was sitting in. It had its own security door that would only open for certain management. It was the reason King knew it was important. Clearly a very important building because it also had three extra cameras on the outside, and Arnie, the other guard on site, made a *face* when he said the word *restricted*. When King asked why, Arnie gave the standard, "above my pay grade," and moved on.

There were four other guards employed at Volkov, but they always worked together in pairs. So King would only see them at shift change. Arnie was his *"partner,"* as Arnie called it. King got the short version of how Arnie had always wanted to be a cop, but because he wasn't one of the "good ole boys" in Barrow, they didn't let him on the force. Therefore, he was relegated to security. A job he takes "very seriously." King smiled thinking about it. Arnie was a good guy, but quirky. As King set on to investigating the Volkov facility as he was sent there to do, he felt he could manipulate Arnie to keep him from interfering. Arnie reminded King of a chubby Barney Fife. His heart was in the right place; it was the rest of him that wasn't.

It was midnight now and all was quiet. Arnie had said that there was usually only one person that would sometimes come in to work at that time of night, but no one ever really knew when. His name was Dr. Semenov, a supposed *oil and natural gas scientist*, but King could tell that Arnie really had no clue. The outer door buzzed and King jumped, not ready for that noise to break the silence.

King moved his head to the monitor watching the main entrance. A white-haired man in a white lab coat was removing a parka as he stared back at him, and King was shook. The last thing he'd expected to see was a familiar face that night, but sure enough, one was looking him right in the eyes.

Dmitry Kuznetsov.

King had studied and memorized the profile of this scientist of infectious diseases and world-renowned virologist before he burned it. Kuznetsov was the central theme of the reason King had been sent to Barrow. And there was no mistaking this man. His nose was big enough to have its own zip code, and his white eyebrows each looked like the hair on a troll doll. He had a very worried look on his face. King was shocked that he would already be able to report back to Sam and President Gibbons that Kuznetsov was in fact in Barrow.

This put King square in the belly of the beast.

Right where he wanted to be.

Kuznetsov shouted into the camera in a Russian accent, "Come on! I haven't got all night!" Then he held up his badge to the camera as if he understood that maybe the new guy wasn't sure of who he was. He seemed as though he was in a hurry.

"X, what are you doing?" Arnie rushed over and pressed the button allowing Kuznetsov to enter the front door.

"Sorry," King said. "Wasn't expecting anyone to buzz in this late."

"Well, this is the exact guy you don't want to piss off. You'll be gone in no time if you do."

Kuznetsov walked through the front entrance, then scanned his ID badge so the internal doors would open. On the computer screen in front of King, the ID card flashed up. It was in fact Kuznetsov's face, but unsurprisingly, his name was different. The badge read Doctor Ivan Semenov. King could feel the adrenaline seeping into his system for the first time since he'd arrived in Barrow. Until that moment, no one was certain that Kuznetsov had disappeared to Alaska; it had only been speculation. Now it was reality. And King was ready to dive headfirst into throwing a wrench in these Commies' plans.

Arnie rushed over to the glass doors that opened when Kuznetsov scanned his badge. "I'm sorry, Dr. Semenov, Xavier is new. It won't happen again."

Kuznetsov walked right by Arnie and stared King down as he passed. "It better not."

"Yes, sir," Arnie said as he chased behind him. "It won't, right, X?"

King didn't speak. Kuznetsov was already on his way through the security door, so there was no reason to. He was walking the hallway to the only building King hadn't been allowed to see, and it didn't surprise King at all—because they weren't studying the land for oil or for gravel extraction; they were building a weapon. An invisible killer that would give the Russians back world power that every American involved in the intelligence community had known they'd been looking to gain since the Cold War.

King felt a hard slap on his shoulder. "Well, you blew that one, didn't you, buddy?" Arnie had a big goofy grin on his face. "Don't worry, I covered for you."

King smiled. "Thanks, Arnie."

"Hey, nice cut on your forehead you got there. I heard you went down like a lead ball off a high table when Ryker hit you."

"How did you already hear about that? It just happened a couple of hours ago."

"Nothing happens here without everyone knowing about it. Especially when the new guy gets pummeled trying to hit on Cali."

"I wasn't hitting on Cali." King put his hands on his hips.

"Well, seems Ryker was definitely hitting on you. Does he hit as hard as they say he does?"

"Aren't there some doors you need to make sure are locked or something?"

"I knew he did. Just glad you're okay. Wouldn't want to lose you before you really even get started."

"I think I'll make it."

"All right," Arnie said. "I'm gonna go check the eastern buildings. Try not to break anything while I'm gone."

"I'll do my best."

As Arnie walked away, King watched the monitor as Kuznetsov walked toward the forbidden door. He didn't know what it was, maybe it was the fact that he was sent to Barrow to investigate that made him long to go through that restricted door, but he really felt it was something even deeper. Something buried in the human DNA that when someone tells you that you can't have or see something, it makes you want it that much more. Either way, King needed to find a way to see what Volkov Mining and Dmitry Kuznetsov were hiding. And he needed to do it fast.

With so much security, and so many cameras focused on that forbidden door, it was going to be near impossible. King was a lot of things, but an expert in evading cameras was not one of them. The viral videos of his efforts in London and his fight with Husaam Hammoud in Athens were perfect examples. He was going to need help. He didn't know anyone in Barrow, but fortunately you don't have to be in the same place to take out digital cameras. He needed a techie.

The good thing was, he and Sam kept one on call: Dbie Johnson.

King glanced over his shoulder to make sure Arnie was

gone. Thankfully he did know enough about video equipment to know how to rewind. He did so until Kuznetsov appeared on the screen again, and paused it when Kuznetsov held his ID badge up to the camera. King pulled out his phone and snapped a picture of the ID. He now at least had proof that Kuznetsov was there in Barrow. And he knew where to go to find what Kuznetsov was working on. The hacking into the cameras part to keep King from being seen would be up to Dbie.

Either way, for the first time since he'd flown into Barrow, King felt like his reason for being there was being realized.

Now all he had to do was stop a deadly global pandemic before it started.

No pressure.

5

WASHINGTON, DC

PRESIDENT BOBBY GIBBONS finished nuking his popcorn and was adding in some dark chocolate chunks. He didn't care much for the chocolate, but his wife, Beth, loved the salty sweet combo. It was rare that the two of them were able to sit down and enjoy a movie together, so he was really looking forward to it. It had been a whirlwind of a year already, and it was only the last of January.

He and Beth were still getting used to their new home. The White House was old, but you wouldn't know it by the living quarters. It had all been remodeled to Beth's specifications before he was sworn in a week ago. The only real request Bobby had was that there was a movie room. Movies had been a way for him to escape ever since he was a kid, and he was excited to take two hours and think of nothing but the story he was being told as he nibbled on some popcorn.

Bobby walked down the hall, and at the end was the movie room. He walked in and Beth had already queued up the movie. The room was basically just a couch and a massive hundred-inch television fixed to the wall in front of it. The sound system was state of the art, something he was ready to put to the test.

"You're sure this is the movie you want to watch?" Beth said. "You may not get another for a while. Aren't these kinda cheesy?"

She was referring to the movie *Fast and the Furious 9*. Last year, amongst the hysteria over COVID-19, all major houses had postponed their releases. This movie wasn't set to come out until April of this year, but being the president does have its perks.

Bobby rounded the couch, leaned down, and kissed her on the lips. She was as beautiful as the day he met her. "Cheesy? Come on. Where's your sense of adventure?"

"You know me, honey, I'd watch a *girly* movie every time. But you don't get to do this often, so this is fine."

"We can watch something else if you want. But then you'd miss Vin Diesel flexing his muscles. I know you like that."

"You don't have to sell me, I really don't care what we watch. I'm here for the popcorn."

"Mmm hmm," Bobby said with a smile.

He took a seat on the plush couch, pressed the button on the side to recline the chair, pressed the button on the remote to dim the lights, and took a satisfied exhale.

"Excited?" Beth smiled as she grabbed some popcorn.

"Very."

Beth pressed play, and the graphic of the earth appeared on the screen with the word UNIVERSAL wrapping around it.

Just as the studio logo disappeared and the first action scene began full throttle, the phone on the wall began to buzz. Bobby's heart sank. He'd instructed everyone to give him an hour unless there was a critical update. Bobby didn't mind the hours that he had to put in to be the president of the United States, but he could already tell what he was going to hate about the most important job in the world: there was rarely good news.

"Just leave it," Beth said.

"I don't have that option anymore, sweetheart."

Beth hit pause and Bobby walked over to the phone.

"Hello."

"Mr. President," his secretary said. "So sorry to bother you, but you're needed in the Oval Office."

"Update on Alaska?"

"Yes, sir. Critical. I'm assuming you haven't seen the news?"

Bobby's stomach turned.

"I haven't."

"Someone leaked the story about the town in Alaska."

"Shit. All right. Be right down."

6

After a quick change of clothes, and a minute to pick popcorn from his teeth, Bobby walked into the Oval Office. His press secretary, the secretary of health and human services, and the secretary's virologist tasked with helping the investigator in Koenig, Alaska, were all waiting for him. They were gathered around a television watching an anchor deliver the news.

"Mr. President," they all said as they stood to greet him.

"Have a seat. Let me see what they're saying."

A graphic of a biohazard symbol was floating beside the man's head as he spoke to the camera. The look on his face was worried. Bobby knew then that the shit was hitting the fan. The use of the biohazard symbol already got his blood boiling. The sensationalism of the media, right and left, made him about as angry as anything in the world. He took a deep breath and listened to the report.

As you know, with everything the world went through with the coronavirus last year, this couldn't be more terrifying. Again, the source has not been confirmed, but the body count in Alaska absolutely has. In case you missed it, an entire town in Alaska mysteriously died last week. All one hundred and three of them. And the report from a city close to them is that it was from some sort of a virus. That's all we know at this time. Please do not panic, but stay tuned as we will be updating this story the second we get more information.

Bobby slammed his fist down on his desk, and the three people in the room all jumped to attention.

"I can't believe this bullshit. Who leaked this story? I want their head on a stake." Bobby walked around his desk and stood directly in front of the three of them. "And can you believe the irresponsibility of that report?" He was shouting. "The source has not been confirmed, but everyone is dead. But don't panic! Just stay tuned!"

Bobby walked away and made a lap around his desk.

"We need to get out in front of this," Linda Morales, his press secretary, said.

"Well no shit!" Bobby turned around and saw the shocked look on Linda's face. He took a deep breath and changed his tone. "Sorry, Linda. That wasn't directed at you."

"I get it. This is bad."

"This is worse than that. After last year, people are going to panic. And with reporting like that, I can't say I blame them."

There was a knock at the door; then it pushed inward. It was his secretary. "CIA Director Lucas here to see you."

Robert walked in, a solemn look on his face.

"Perfect timing," Bobby said.

"Mr. President," Robert acknowledged.

"We have to issue a statement," the press secretary urged.

"Any suggestions, Andrew?" Bobby looked at his secretary of health.

Donna Ingram—the virologist—spoke instead. "You could say their water was tainted. Wouldn't be the first time something like that has happened in a rural area."

"I can't lie to the American people."

It was his knee-jerk reaction.

"Can you afford not to, sir?" Robert said.

Bobby was quiet for a moment. He really didn't want to lie to the people. But with the kind of irresponsible reporting that was going in the media, they had almost forced his hand. He knew that every president at some point in their time in office dealt with this sort of thing, but that didn't make it any easier. He was going to have to develop thicker skin.

His press secretary cleared her throat. "If it makes you feel better, I can allude to the fact that the water tainting is just one of the possibilities we are investigating. And that there is no evidence yet that this was viral."

"Okay," Bobby said. "I like that better. Let's calm people down." Then he looked at Robert. "And I want to know who leaked this, you hear me? Right. Now."

"I'll get on it," Robert said. "In the meantime, I just received an update and we need to talk in private."

Bobby looked at everyone else in the room. "You heard him. Can we please have the room?"

"Of course," Andrew said, "But we were here for a reason, Donna has an update from Koenig."

"Go on."

"We've had the first death," the virologist said, getting right to it. "And many others are losing the fight with whatever virus was unleashed on them."

Bobby couldn't believe his ears. This was really happening. Someone was weaponizing a virus, and he had no idea if they'd already brought it to the lower forty-eight states.

Donna continued. "This one is worse than the first town, Mr. President."

"How?"

"Because the incubation period is much longer. And the beginning symptoms were barely that of the common cold."

Bobby understood what that meant, but he wanted confirmation. "So someone can not only infect a lot of other people before they even know they're sick, but they think all that is wrong with them is just a common cold?"

"Yes. And according to my virologist in Koenig—the only person there not infected—it's the perfect virus to weaponize because of that. And the fact that only just a couple of days after very mild symptoms, it morphs into this killing machine inside the infected person's body. Quickly taking them from okay to dead."

"So everyone will think they have a cold—"

"Then they will drop dead." Donna was blunt.

It was clear there was no time to waste. "Okay, please let Robert and me have the room. I want an update every fifteen minutes."

"Yes, Mr. President."

Everyone but Robert left the Oval Office.

"Okay Robert. Please give me some good news."

Bobby went back behind his desk and took his seat. Robert sat down across from him.

"Alexander King checked in with Sam and was able to confirm that Dmitry Kuznetsov is in fact at the Volkov Mining company under an alias."

Bobby's mood lifted. "This is fantastic news."

"It is. He is awaiting your instruction."

"Well, hell, Robert, you're the director of the CIA. You know more about this than anyone. What's the next move?"

"That depends." Robert sat forward in his chair. "We can send in a team and shut the entire facility down. Or we can wait . . . and watch."

"Okay. I'm assuming you mean wait to see if we can get to who is responsible."

Robert nodded.

"But I have to keep the American people safe," Bobby said as he sat back in his chair, trying to think it through.

"Look, we can shut this facility down in a matter of hours. King could take Kuznetsov down tonight."

"I feel a *but* coming on," Bobby said.

"*But* . . . I don't think that would stop anything. We don't know enough yet. While whoever is building this virus might very well be doing it in Barrow at the Volkov facility, that doesn't mean they have kept everything there. I can almost guarantee you they have already sent samples back to wherever this entire thing is being orchestrated."

"So shutting down the facility and killing Kuznetsov might not actually stop anything," Bobby said.

"Right. I would almost guarantee that whatever strain of this virus was tested in Koenig is already in the hands of someone who can distribute it. And that isn't in Barrow, Alaska."

"I agree. So what is the next move?"

"I know it doesn't feel right to just sit on this, with so many Americans in danger, but we have to let King do some more digging in Barrow. And maybe just as important, we have to let Sam run down where this thing is ultimately being concocted. We need to know if Russia is planning to start World War III with a bioweapon or not."

Bobby couldn't believe this is what his first few days in the White House were consisting of. Possibly the biggest threat to America since its inception. But clearly the threat was real. If for no other reason, he could see it on Robert's face.

"So you think it's Russia," Bobby said. "How confident are you?"

"Confident enough that Sam has already been there for a week. And I think she may have found out just who Kuznetsov is communicating with in Moscow."

Bobby thought about it for a moment. "Shouldn't we have King in Moscow if you think that is the epicenter?"

"I think Sam is every bit as good as King. And right now we need King in Barrow. They could just as easily distribute the virus from there. All we can do is hope they haven't already."

Bobby swallowed hard. He had a long night ahead of him. After the coronavirus outbreak, the sitting president had been good about making sure there was a strong pandemic team in place in case this happened again. It was time for Bobby to make sure they were getting prepared. He wasn't going to let this thing get away from him. And he just hoped the agents in place could do the same.

"Okay. It's settled then," Bobby stood. "We wait . . . and pray we haven't made a monumental mistake."

7

SAM HARRISON SIDLED up to a row of boxes piled seven feet high inside the hangar. As she pulled her Glock from her concealed hip holster, she was hoping she hadn't overextended herself. She had to gain some information about what was going on with the virus here in Russia, *if* something was actually happening. As she peered through a crack in the boxes at the private portion of the Domodedovo Airport in southeastern Moscow, she felt certain it could be a matter of millions of people living or dying. All her instincts from her days in MI6 and with the CIA, running down baddies with Alexander King, were telling her that this could be her first real lead. Some answers would be found here.

Up until two hours ago, Sam had been spinning her wheels a bit in Russia. She had located the famous virologist Dmitry Kuznetsov's protégé, Veronika Kamenev, and even learned she'd been seen meeting with some of the higher-ups in the Russian government. However, none of that was concrete evidence that Veronika was involved with anything Kuznetsov might possibly be doing with weaponizing a virus.

Things were completely different now.

Sam had zero question whether Veronika was involved with Kuznetsov. And the only reason that was the case was due to sheer luck. Intel from an agent-in-place in Moscow led Sam to a meeting between Veronika and a supposed agent for the Foreign Intelligence Service, or FIS, the Russian equivalent of the CIA. It wasn't anything that Sam found out by being a few tables away from the meeting. In fact, she hadn't understood a word of what little she could hear. They were speaking Russian. The point of luck was that Sam actually knew the person Veronika was meeting with. And Sam knew she was not Russian intelligence because she used to be a part of Reign, Alexander King and Sam's clandestine team in the CIA that was disbanded a couple of years ago when Alexander King was forced to fake his own death.

Sam couldn't believe her eyes when she'd watched Zhanna Dragov walk into the cafe. Sure, she was Russian, and Sam *was* in Moscow, but last she'd heard about Zhanna was that she'd fallen in love and subsequently fallen off the grid.

Looks like that had been just a cover.

Sam had managed to follow the two of them all the way from the city center to the airport. Zhanna had been ushered into the same vehicle as Veronika, and Sam couldn't imagine how Zhanna had become involved with what she and Alexander were trying to run down there in Russia.

Zhanna hadn't changed a bit. She and Sam were built a lot alike. Five feet eight, athletic, fit, but not overly muscular. However, the similarities ended there. As Zhanna was talking to Veronika at the other end of the hangar, her fiery red hair sparked in the yellow overhead lights. To the left of them, the hangar door rattled and began to open. Though Sam was tucked in a corner behind some boxes, she was still exposed. There was a door behind her, and if someone came through now, she would be forced to fight. That was the last thing she wanted to do.

Beyond Zhanna and Veronika, standing beside a small propeller plane, there were three men. Sam didn't see any guns, but there was little question in her mind that they were strapped. As the hangar door continued to rise, Sam could hear a plane approaching from the runway. She crouched even further and found a different slot to peep through. Everyone's attention was now on the jet that was pulling to a stop just outside the hangar. As the engine shut down and the cold air seeped into the open room, Sam sat motionless, listening.

Three men exited the jet and walked inside the hangar. The man in front was carrying a briefcase. The two behind him looked like the muscle. The massive door clicked and began to roll down. Before it disappeared from sight, Sam took a mental picture of the tail number on the plane, just in case it could be helpful later: Z450XY. The hangar was about two hundred feet long and about half as deep. Sam would easily be able to hear everything being said. She would also be entirely caught in the cross fire if anything were to go wrong. Since she had no idea the nature of this meeting, she remained open to all possibilities.

"Who is she?" the front man for the trio barked as he pointed to Zhanna. His accent was Asian, and as he stepped into the light, Sam could see that he was in fact from somewhere in the Far East. Things were getting more complicated by the second.

Veronika took a step forward. "Do you have the samples or not?"

Samples? Alarms rang in Sam's head. She obviously had no clue what they were talking about, but it sounded like things might be lining up.

"I was told that you would be the only one here," the man said. "Open the door, we're leaving."

Veronika looked back over her shoulder at the three men standing guard. At the same time, Sam watched Zhanna slide her right arm around her back. Whatever this was supposed to be, it was about to go sideways. Sam edged to the end of the boxes and readied her gun. Her only immediate concern was making sure that Zhanna stayed alive. She could give a damn about the rest of these people.

"I'm not opening the door," Veronika said. Her men all brandished handguns at the same time. "Hand over the briefcase. Then you are free to go."

If everyone started shooting, there was no way Zhanna was going to make it out of there. Sam took in her surroundings. She looked beyond everyone at the back wall of the hangar: nothing useful. Off to her left were some random storage boxes. As she glanced up at the hanging lights above them, out of the corner of her eye she noticed the two men behind the guy with the briefcase as they moved their arms.

This was going down.

Sam turned her gun toward the ceiling and fired a couple of shots at one of the hanging lights. The sound of her gunfire echoed in the open hangar, and the sizzle of the ruined light sparked above them. Sam had given Zhanna her window to find cover, and as Sam dropped to her stomach behind the boxes, she hoped when she popped back up that she would find Zhanna had taken advantage of the opportunity.

In a blink, the quiet hangar sounded like a war zone as a hailstorm of gunfire erupted. The boxes in front of Sam took some hits, and so too did the wall behind her. Through a small break in the boxes, she watched as Zhanna fired at the three men behind her from a prone position on the ground. Sam slid herself over to the left side of the boxes and fired on the men who had come into the hangar from the plane. One of them dropped from her shots, and the other beside him went down from someone else's gun.

The gunfire stopped. Sam popped up to a crouched position. She needed to take inventory of who was left. Then she heard a woman's voice shout something in Russian. Sam didn't know what was said, but Zhanna's raspy voice was unmistakable.

Sam peeked above the boxes. Gunshots came her way. Sam was able to see that there was no one left standing in that hangar.

"Zhanna! Stop shooting!"

Everything went quiet. Sam finally located Zhanna ducked beneath the wing of the prop plane.

"Is everyone dead?" Sam asked.

"Not yet," Zhanna said. Her Russian accent seemed less

heavy than when Sam last spoke to her a couple of years ago. "How do you know my name?"

"Zhanna, it's Sam Harrison. I'm coming out. Don't shoot."

Sam stepped out from behind the boxes. Zhanna duck-walked out from under the wing of the plane, her gun still pointed in Sam's direction.

"Sam?" Zhanna finally recognized her and pulled her gun down by her side. "What are you doing here?"

"Was going to ask you the same thing."

As Sam began walking toward her, something caught Zhanna's attention and she whipped her head in the direction of Veronika lying on the ground. Sam jogged over and watched Zhanna crouch beside Veronika as she picked up her phone. Zhanna hit the speaker button and gave Sam the index finger to the lips.

"Veronika!" a man shouted from the phone; then the line went dead.

"She had someone phoned in during the entire thing," Zhanna said. "We must go. Now."

8

BARROW, ALASKA, 9:00 A.M.

A POUNDING sound pulled King from the dark depths of sleep. His eyes shot open yet found nothing but black. He slid his hand under his pillow to grab his Glock as he rolled to a sitting position and grabbed his phone. The time was nine, but since it was pitch-black in the room, he was still confused. The knock came again and snapped him to his feet. He rushed over to the window at the front of his small rental. He pulled back the blackout curtain, and as he looked at what seemed to be twilight, it all flooded back to him: where he was and why it was dark at nine in the morning.

King shifted to his right and could see the back of a winter coat standing outside his front door. Though it had occurred to him he was in Alaska, the implications of opening the door in his underwear had not. Suddenly standing in front of him was Cali, bundled in a winter coat.

The sting of the subzero wind against his bare chest nearly knocked him backward. Cali rushed forward and slammed the door behind her.

"Still not used to living in Alaska, I see." Cali's face was covered by a black bandana, but he could tell by the shape her eyes took that she was smiling. Most likely laughing at the noob new to town.

King kept the gun behind his back as he backpedaled toward the couch. He had no clothing in sight, so he was going to have to indulge the awkward moment.

"You can put the gun down. I'm not going to hurt you."

King gave her a sheepish grin and revealed the gun. "Sorry. I was disoriented."

"Is it a habit where you're from to grab a gun when someone knocks on your door?"

King had to think fast. "No, but when someone threatens you at a bar the night before, and you're new to town, you really don't know what might happen."

Cali took down her fluffy hood and removed the bandana from her face. She was beautiful. Her smile was enough to warm the cold air that had blown in. "Makes sense, and that's why I'm here actually. To apologize for what happened."

"Mind if I put on some clothes?"

"If you must."

She was flirting. At least he thought she was. A couple of years ago King would have already pulled some one-liners in an attempt to be charming. It had been a while, and he was off his game. Faking your death, living in hiding, and chasing terrorists can often get in the way of your sex life.

"I think I must." King walked into the bedroom and tucked the gun back under the pillow. He grabbed a long-sleeved tee from a pile on the desk in the corner and threw on some joggers.

"You didn't have to come by," he said, raising his voice so she could hear from the other room. "What happened last night wasn't your fault." King checked his hair in the mirror. Though it was a bit longer than he would have liked, his thick brown hair was rarely out of place, even after sleep. He ran his fingers through it and walked back out into the living room.

"I woke you up, didn't I?"

"Yeah, I'm on night shift, so I just got to bed a bit ago."

Cali buried her head in her hands, then looked up with an embarrassed smile. "I'm so sorry. I just added insult to injury."

"It's fine. I have some things to do anyway. Glad you came by."

"Maybe this will help."

Cali reached inside her coat and produced a brown paper sack. It was shaped an awful lot like a bottle. She extended it, and he took it in his hands.

"I don't know much about bourbon," she said, "but they said this was a good one. They threw it in on our order last time."

King pulled the bottle from the bag. He couldn't believe it: it was one of his favorites. "George T. Stagg? They just threw this in on your order?"

"Why, is it a good one?"

She really didn't know. "It is. And one of my favorites."

"Well, good. Glad I could give you a little piece of home."

"It's not necessary, but thank you." King walked over to the small kitchen behind him and set the bottle on the stove. "Can I get you some coffee? It's shitty, but it's the only thing I have to offer so you'll stay a little longer."

He looked over his shoulder and watched as she removed her coat. King was trying to remember that he was once a charming bachelor. Maybe he still had a little game left. But it was hard to woo a woman in the shack he was currently living in, decorated with none of his own things, and in a land that was as foreign to him as a country song on pop radio.

"You kidding? I live on shitty coffee."

King poured some preground beans into the coffee maker and filled the pot with water. He grabbed some strawberries from the fridge and spread them on a cutting board with a knife. He set the board on the small two-person dining table that separated the kitchen from the living room. "It isn't the Beverly Hilton, but it's what I've got."

Cali took a seat. "You've been to LA?"

"I have. It's not really my cup of tea, but I don't mind south of the city."

King used to have a place on the beach in San Diego. But that was a lifetime ago. Before he'd let go of his civilian life entirely.

"Really? I grew up in San Diego. My family moved to LA when my mother became a surgeon at Cedars-Sanai. It's not exactly my vibe either."

King grabbed the coffee pot and set down two mugs. "So were you running from something, too, when you came here?" He poured them both a cup. "You did say that's what people do when they move to Barrow."

She gave him a wry smile. "You could say my dad and I both were. My mom was killed trying to save a gang member's life after we witnessed a drive-by shooting. They killed her for trying to help the man live."

King knew all there was to know about loss. He wanted to relate with her, with any human at this point, but especially the pretty woman sitting at his table. He wasn't sure what the rules were for sharing family history when undercover, but the urge to feel *something* with *someone* took precedent over what he thought was a small detail in a much larger life.

"I'm sorry. My mother was shot in front of me as well."

"You're kidding."

"I'm not. I was only fifteen."

She moved her hand from her mug to his hand and gave it a squeeze. "The hurt never goes away, does it?"

He shook his head.

"How did you deal with the pain?"

That portion of his history was not sharable. It's a good story, but not one he could elaborate on with her. Burying your pain in the dead bodies of bad guys was an odd way to go, but for King it was the only thing that helped him cope with missing his parents.

He decided to lighten the mood. "Though it might not have seemed like it last night, I got into a lot of fights after my mom died."

Cali smiled and gave him a wink. Then she took a shot at him. "Yeah? You're right, it didn't seem like it."

King laughed. He was glad to receive the jab. Sam would have approved. With that thought he immediately checked his phone that was lying on the table beside him. No notifications. Sam should have checked in by now. As much as he wanted to be in the moment, the thought of Sam in trouble pulled him out of it.

"I'm sorry, it was just a joke," Cali said as she took her hand away.

"What?" King looked back up at her. When he saw concern on her face, it snapped him back to the conversation. "No, sorry. Believe me, I appreciate a good ribbing. Especially when I deserve it. I was just supposed to hear from someone and haven't yet. No big deal."

"Natalie?"

King raised an eyebrow, then remembered he'd mentioned Natalie last night as the girl he'd come to Alaska to forget. "Oh, no. She's a distant memory."

A memory he couldn't shake, but distant nonetheless.

"Good." That smile again. Flecks of green flared in her hazel eyes.

It wasn't often that he was with a woman so comfortable in her own skin to forgo makeup, but in Cali's case, she must have known she didn't need it.

"Sorry I got so deep so fast," Cali said. "I'm not one to beat around the bush."

"No problem," he said. "I can appreciate that. You need any cream or sugar?"

"How 'bout some of that whiskey?"

King smiled. "You ever met anyone from Kentucky?"

"Not sure really. Why? I say something wrong?"

"A couple of things actually."

She squinted her eyes at him. "Do tell, Mister Manners."

"It's just that if it's bourbon we're talking about, we would always call it bourbon. Not whiskey. Because to us there is a difference. And bourbon like George T. Stagg? You don't go wasting that by mixing it with coffee. Mixing it with anything, for that matter."

"Well, X, I'm so sorry to have trampled your heritage."

They both laughed. Then he went back to the kitchen cabinet, opened it, and pulled out a bottle of Canadian whiskey. "Now *this* stuff? It's good for mixing."

"Don't you lose your Kentucky card for buying a bottle like that?"

King feigned a look of being appalled. "Oh no, darlin', I didn't buy this. Whoever was here before me left it behind. And I don't blame them. But it will work in the coffee."

"I'm just glad you didn't tell me that it's five o'clock somewhere, like every other cliché American would."

"I'm a lot of things, Cali," he said as he poured some whiskey into both of their coffee cups, "but cliché isn't one of them."

"Yeah?" She took a sip. So did he. "I noticed that. You're in awfully good shape for no good reason. You ex-military?"

"I am. It's ingrained in the DNA at this point."

King was entranced by Cali. She had that certain way about her. The way she drew him in with her eyes and left him hanging with that smile. But as with everything in King's life, even a moment like this couldn't sustain his full attention. The more time went by, the more his concern grew for Sam. She wasn't the type to be late for anything. Especially checking in with him.

King checked his phone once again.

"If there's something you need to be doing, I can go."

Before he could respond, a horn blasted from the road. Five long and drawn-out beeps.

"Expecting someone?" Cali said.

"No," King told her as he stood from the table.

"Sounds like someone's expecting you."

43

9

As Sam walked over to Zhanna, she motioned for Zhanna to hand over Veronika's phone. Whoever was listening in on the other end of Veronika's phone during this transaction gone bad in the hangar, Sam *had* to learn their identity. Zhanna obliged and Sam checked the phone's screen. It was an unknown number.

"Veronika!" a man with an American accent shouted.

To hear an American's voice come from the phone while she was standing around a pile of bodies in a private hangar in Moscow, Russia, was a bit of a shock to Sam's system. She covered the phone and handed it back to Zhanna. She mouthed to Zhanna to speak in Russian. Zhanna understood. She took the phone and said one sentence in her native tongue. It was enough to help whoever was on the other end of that call to end it immediately.

"They hang up," Zhanna said as she switched back to her broken English.

"Shit." Sam took the phone and pocketed it for later. She took in the carnage around her and moved over toward the briefcase. Though it didn't go down like she had hoped, Zhanna was alive, she had a phone that she hoped she could connect to something of importance, and the briefcase lying on the ground just to her left could fully change the entire complexion of the problems at hand. All in all, it was a win.

"Yes, it is shit," Zhanna said. "But worse shit is coming if we don't leave now."

Sam knew Zhanna was right. "Before we get split up, give me your number." Sam pulled out her phone as Zhanna rattled off some numbers. She pressed call so Zhanna would have her number stored as well. "Why don't you grab that briefcase and I'll see if we have any company outside."

Zhanna gave her a nod, and Sam walked back toward the side door she'd used earlier. On her way, she ejected her mostly empty magazine and replaced it with a full one. It was a good thing she did. Just as she was within a few feet of the door, the pewter handle moved downward. Sam jumped to the spot on the wall where the door was opening toward. She saw the end of a pistol move inside.

Sam grabbed the barrel of the pistol and pushed it to the right as she ducked and shot the man in the knee. She had to go to the floor with him, because there were three more men in military fatigues coming toward her, only about ten feet away.

Military fatigues?

Sam's mind raced as she hit the ground. Her plan of

shooting the man in the knee to keep him alive for questioning was immediately out the window. Now her focus was survival. As she landed face-to-face with the man she'd shot, his eyes were wide with surprise as the two of them bounced off the ground nose to nose, she pulled her gun up and shot him in the stomach.

"Find a back way out!" Sam shouted at Zhanna.

She was able to use the large man as a springboard, digging the right toe of her shoe into his belt and sliding her body along the floor to avoid the shots the men with him fired just before the door slammed shut in their face. Her first instinct was to scramble fast enough to get to the door and lock it. But if she wasn't quick enough, they'd beat her there and shoot her dead. So she popped up to her feet, ran around the boxes back toward the dead bodies she'd already helped lay to rest, and sprinted over to Zhanna whose back was running around the prop plane.

"This way!" Zhanna shouted.

The door behind Sam exploded inward. A cascade of bullets followed, and the loud bangs echoed through the hangar. Sam jumped the body of the man who'd once held the briefcase, and she surged past the plane. The aluminum was filling with holes from the ammo being expensed behind her. She didn't have time to worry about the same damage filling her back. She just had to run.

In front of her, a different door silhouetted Zhanna with bright light. It was dark out, but the light shining down on her made her glow. Before Sam could feel any sense of relief, Zhanna was already shooting around the door at the men in military gear. Whoever it was, whether the actual Russian military or some sort of mercenary team, they weren't commissioned by the American voice Sam had heard coming through Veronika's phone. This team of gunmen had already been at the hangar waiting, either to intercept this briefcase exchange or to shut it down. Regardless, Sam and Zhanna were trapped.

Zhanna fired a few more times and then jumped back inside the hangar, swinging the metal door shut as bullets clanked against it.

"How many?" Sam shouted as gunfire continued behind her.

"Two, maybe more!" Zhanna wasn't rattled yet, but she was on her way there.

The two of them crouched. The prop plane on one side and a thin wall on the other were the only two things keeping them alive. Sam scanned the area around her. On the back wall there were more boxes, and beside them, a pushback tractor. None of it useful. As she scanned back toward the hangar door, she fired a couple of rounds in the direction of the men who were shooting at them from behind the stack of boxes on the other side. If the men outside the door on her right were trained, as long as they were firing they wouldn't enter the hangar for fear of friendly fire. This was her and Zhanna's only window.

Sam took the briefcase from Zhanna and moved toward the door. The men on the other side of the hangar finally stopped shooting. They shouted something in Russian. Sam assumed it was some iteration of *"Don't move,"* but she couldn't worry about that.

Sam looked back at Zhanna as she placed her hand on the door handle. "When I show the briefcase, I need you to shout in Russian that we surrender and tell them to take the briefcase. Tell them to spare us and take what they came for."

Zhanna didn't protest or ask questions. She knew Sam was baiting them. Sam cracked the door open and shoved the briefcase out into the cold air. Zhanna shouted in Russian, a man shouted back, and Zhanna followed with something else that even in Russian sounded like Zhanna was pleading with them. The men shouted once again behind them from the other side of the hangar, but Sam was focused forward out the door, waiting for one of the men to make a move for the briefcase.

Sam reached her hand back and whispered, "Your gun!" Zhanna handed the gun to Sam, and Sam tossed it out the door toward the briefcase. Zhanna shouted something else to the men. Everything went still. Sam raised her Glock in front of her. She could hear the squeak of shoes on the polished floor behind them. The men on the other side of the boxes inside the hangar were coming her way. Zhanna pleaded again, but the men were closing in behind them. They were going to have to make a move whether it was the right time or not.

Then, finally, outside the crack in the door, a hand reached out and grabbed for the briefcase. Sam squeezed the trigger and shot the handle. As the man jerked his hand back, she shoved the door open with her foot and put two in the man's chest, then dove out from behind the open door. As her left side hit the pavement, she shot three more times, hitting the second man twice. As he dropped to the ground, gunfire erupted from inside the hangar, and Zhanna came diving to the ground behind her. Sam jumped up, picked up the briefcase and Zhanna's gun, and handed the gun to her like a relay sprinter passing the baton, and both of them were off and running.

They rounded the front of the hangar and darted right,

toward the parking lot. Sam had no idea what she might find there, but there was no alternative. The airport was encapsulated by a barbed wire fence. Their only way out was through the main gate. Sam glanced over her shoulder, and three men came tripping out the side door. She fired two defensive shots when her Glock locked back. Zhanna picked up Sam's slack by firing a few of her own as Sam exchanged the empty magazine for a fresh one and racked the slide. It was her last spare.

Sam and Zhanna raced around the corner of the building as bullets came flying their way. Sam was barely able to dive behind a van before the first of another string of gunfire was able to hit her, coming from somewhere in the parking lot in front of her. Zhanna made it behind the van unscathed as well, but now the two of them were trapped once again.

As gunshots rang out on the other side of the van and sirens blared in the distance, three men were about to round the corner behind them, leaving them nowhere to run. With their asses on the ground and backs to the van, Sam watched as Zhanna loaded a fresh magazine into her Sig Sauer. All they had left was twenty-four bullets and a prayer.

Sam sucked in a breath of cold Russian air as she set the briefcase down beside her. As the chaos swirled all around them, she desperately tried to control her own breathing. There was no need for conversation, no time either. But she found comfort when she glanced over and Zhanna looked her in the eyes. She saw in Zhanna what she felt deep in her own gut, that she wasn't afraid to fight. The two of them raised their weapons and waited for their enemies.

It didn't take long.

10

BARROW, ALASKA, 9:00 A.M.

KING SET down his coffee and rose from the table. There was a shout from outside his door, but he couldn't make out the words. Only that it was a man's voice. He walked over to the window and raised the blinds.

"Oh Christ, not again," Cali said beside him.

King was looking at a man about ten feet from his door whose arms were raised out from his sides. King couldn't tell who it was by looking, but he knew immediately that it was Ryker after Cali's remark. There were two trucks pulled in behind him, a couple of men in each truck.

"Come on out, boy! I've got a housewarming gift for you!" Ryker shouted.

Cali let go of the blinds and walked over to her coat. "Just let me handle this asshole. The biggest problem with living in the middle of nowhere is that there is nothing to do. This dummy fights out of boredom."

A wave of regret washed over King as he watched Cali hurry into her boots and her coat. He was kicking himself for ever setting foot in that bar, giving this moron outside a chance to cause him trouble. All of this was the last thing he needed. Sam would both laugh and be furious with him if she were there. She'd predicted that a woman in a bar could bring the entire country down if King were enticed. All he could do now was his best to make sure this little side problem didn't become a much larger one. However, that was the reason for the regret. He'd already seen Ryker push Cali once. If he put his hands on her again, there would be no staying out of it. It just wasn't in King's nature.

"Just let him go away, Cali," King said.

"You don't know Ryker," she said as she pulled her beanie down over her ears. "His ego is so big, he won't stop until it's satisfied. And right now he thinks you're the reason he got arrested last night."

"Arrested?" King said.

"Yeah, after the bar cleared out, some of those Russian guys took offense to Ryker getting them kicked out. They went at it in subzero temperatures. Smarts weren't exactly involved. Anyway, I know Ryker, he has to have someone to blame it on."

"And the new guy makes for a good scapegoat."

"You got it. I'll get rid of him, but I'm not sure he'll back off."

"I don't want any trouble. I'm just here to do my job and earn a little money."

Cali raised her eyebrow as she studied him. "You aren't here running from the law, are you? Is that why you're so worried about causing trouble?"

King didn't answer. He'd much rather have her believe

he was a criminal than have her get any ideas about why he was really there. The silence was getting awkward. Finally, horns blowing and Ryker calling King out again broke the intense moment.

"Just stay inside, okay?" Cali said. "I don't need you getting busted up again. You're too pretty for it."

This was a new experience for King, and a hard one to swallow. Watching a woman walk out the door to defend him was as backward as it could get for a Southern gentleman. Especially one who was used to doing the fighting. But he knew, if there was any way she could get Ryker to leave without an incident, that was by far the best scenario. Even if it bought King only a day.

Cali opened the door and walked out. King grabbed his coat from the hook and threw it on as he walked over to the window. Cali hadn't shut the door all the way, so King was able to hear their conversation.

"What the hell are you doing here? You're not into this guy, are you?" Ryker said. His voice was animated.

"What I do is none of your business." Cali got right in Ryker's face. She was a spitfire. "Never has been, never will be. Now why don't you and your redneck friends just get the hell out of here. Don't any of you have jobs?"

Ryker turned his attention from Cali to the house. "She's fighting your battles again, bro," he called out. "What kind of pansy are you?"

All King could do was shake his head. In his experience, most guys like Ryker who actually knew how to fight weren't always trying to get into them. But sometimes, when the good old days pass a guy like him by, it becomes the only thing he is known for. It was clear to King that fighting was Ryker's identity, and it was the only one he had. And

King had a terrible feeling Ryker wasn't going to leave until he got a fight.

"Just don't touch her," King said under his breath as he watched through the window.

Outside in the twilight, Ryker tried to step around Cali, but she shuffled over and got in his way.

"This doesn't concern you anymore, Cali. Move, or I'll move you!"

On reflex, King's fists clenched.

"You have no beef with him, Ryker." Cali was trying to reason with him, but you can't reason with stupid. "It's not his fault you got arrested. It's your fault you're just a punch-drunk loser who lives in the past."

King winced. Her approach, while well intended, was only going to provoke a guy like Ryker.

"Come on out! Fight like a man!"

Ryker tried to step around Cali again, and again she moved. This was humiliating for King, but he *had* to keep the big picture in mind. And this douchebag had nothing to do with what was important.

"Just go, Ryker!"

"Look, Cali, either move, or I'll move you! I'm not playing!"

King zipped up his coat and slid into his boots. This was happening. He glanced up at the trucks behind Ryker to confirm that there were only four other men. His breaths were quickening as he watched. And just as he thought, Cali didn't back down. Ryker moved, and she moved right in front of him. Ryker wrapped both his hands around Cali's shoulders, picked her up, and tossed her about three feet down to the ground. She landed on her ass in the dusting of snow, and her momentum carried her backward hard enough that she smacked the back of her head on the ground.

King whipped the door open and took a step out the door. Clouds of steam were puffing from his mouth as the adrenaline hurried his breath.

"Looks like you got what you wanted," King said. "Hate to tell you, but it's not going to be what you're expecting."

A cold wind blew across King's bare face. But as Ryker stepped forward and into a fighting stance, the only thing he felt was the burn of anger moving all through him.

11

THE THREE MEN who were chasing after Sam and Zhanna from inside the hangar were at least smart enough to stop at the edge of the building and assess where the two women had gone. There also were bullets flying their way from the opposite side of the parking lot, which Sam had no choice but to assume was friendly fire for them. But really, she had no idea. Clearly what was in the briefcase by her side was of incredible importance, so there could certainly be more than one faction vying for it.

There was a car blocking Sam and Zhanna from the men who had stopped at the side of the hangar. For the moment they were covered. Whoever was behind them had now stopped firing. Sam took the quiet moment to check the briefcase. When she'd accidentally shot the handle, it had broken the lock. She opened the briefcase and inside were four vials full of a mostly clear liquid, two with green tops, two with blue. No instructions or guide was given inside. All of them were marked with a different number, none of which meant anything to Sam. She removed the four vials and handed the two with blue tops to Zhanna.

"We need to split up," Sam whispered. "If these are as important as they seem, we can't chance them getting us both and having all the vials. We need to know what is inside them."

Sam could tell by the worried look on Zhanna's face that she didn't like the idea of splitting up. But it only took a second for Zhanna to realize Sam's logic, and she confirmed the plan with a nod.

Sam stole a glance over the trunk of the car in front of her. She immediately ducked her head back down when one of the men at the corner of the hangar fired at her. Zhanna tucked two of the vials in her pocket, and Sam did the same.

"I'll cover you until you find a car with keys," Sam said. Then she pointed at the barbed wire fence on their right. There was a patch of grass beyond it, then the road. "Drive right through the fence there, then switch cars as soon as you can. Call Robert Lucas at CIA headquarters, and he'll get you in touch with me."

"I can't just leave you here," Zhanna said.

Someone yelled something in Chinese behind them. Though the men had Sam and Zhanna trapped, they were growing impatient.

"You don't have a choice," Sam said. "When I start shooting, you start running. There is no other way out."

Zhanna lifted up and glanced through the window at the men behind them. "I see two. And there were three coming out of the hangar. There is no way you make it out alive."

Sam rechecked her last magazine, loaded it back into her Glock, then racked the slide. "Just run when I start shooting, and don't look back."

Zhanna hung her head. "You and Xander are more alike than you think."

Sam gave her a wink, then focused on the corner of the hangar. "Go!" She raised up and shot twice, bouncing two bullets off the aluminum siding of the hangar. Zhanna was off and running. Then Sam whipped around and fired at the two men Zhanna said were behind her, then immediately turned to shoot at the hangar again. The men behind her fired, and when she went to turn, shots came from the men hiding behind the hangar wall, busting the glass of the car beside her. Sam pulled the lock up inside the broken window and cracked open the door as she ducked down. She closed the briefcase, shouted as loud as she could, "Don't shoot! Take the briefcase!" and tossed it out in the parking lot where all the gunmen could see.

Sam crawled inside the Cadillac sedan, did a quick search for keys, but came up empty. She heard a car start in the distance. She prayed it was Zhanna and that her distraction had worked.

"Just take the briefcase!" Sam shouted again as she slid back out of the car.

She had eight rounds left in her magazine and no way out. Then she heard screeching tires. When she looked off to her right, Zhanna was plowing through the fence just as Sam had asked her to. The added bonus of distracting the men hiding behind the hangar wall was the window Sam needed in order to stand a chance. She rounded the back of the Cadillac, away from the men at the hangar who were now firing at Zhanna's vehicle. The two men who had trapped her on the opposite side were running for the briefcase. Sam raised her gun and fired twice at the man in front. He dropped to the ground, but the man behind her had been running with his gun up to cover him, and he got off three shots before Sam could duck behind the next car in the lot.

Pain exploded in her left shoulder as she spun and dropped to the ground. She'd been hit, but she still had her wits about her. As she lay on the snow-dusted pavement, she could see beneath the car beside her, and she watched the man who'd shot her grab the briefcase. Then, to her surprise, the men who'd given chase inside the hangar and had just been firing at Zhanna in her getaway car, began firing at the man who'd just shot her. There definitely were two different organizations at the airport looking for the briefcase. What the hell did she have in her pocket that so many people not only knew about but were willing to shoot over without question? Could this many people know about the supposed secret virus? Could this have come from Barrow, Alaska?

Sam lay on the cold pavement without moving. Her shoulder was throbbing in pain. The man with the briefcase was still running away, firing behind him at the three men giving chase. For the moment, they had forgotten about her. Ironically, getting shot may have just saved her life.

12

"Ryker!" Cali shouted. She was still on her ass where he had shoved her to the ground. "Just leave him alone! He did nothing to you!"

Cali's shouts fell on deaf ears. King watched Ryker take two steps forward. While he didn't know what kind of boxer Ryker had been, King could tell by Ryker's personality that he was used to being the aggressor. And the sheriff had told him that Ryker hit like a truck, which King could attest to after being punched by him in the face. So he was used to overpowering and stalking his opponents. It was also clear from last night at the bar that Ryker's right hand was his power punch. That's why when King took a couple of steps of his own, he began to circle to Ryker's left, moving away from his best punch.

What Ryker had yet to understand was that there was no way he could win this fight. Not because he wasn't a better boxer than King, but because he was merely a boxer. He had only three, maybe four tools to work with, at best. Immediately after King's parents were murdered, when King was just fifteen years old, he became obsessed with learning every skill that could be useful if he ever got the chance to find who'd taken his family from him. He had studied all forms of combat. Boxing—so he was good with his hands. Muay Thai—so he could also strike with elbows, knees, and kicks. And Brazilian Jiu Jitsu—so if he met his match on his feet, he could always take the fight to the ground. Ryker fighting against King was like a golfer only having one club for the entire course. No matter how good he was with that one club, he wasn't going to fair well against someone with a full bag.

On top of that, someone trained in the way King had been trained—both throughout his childhood, then even more refined in the Navy SEALs and Special Operations—also had fight and combat IQ. This could help him calculate far beyond the one-on-one fight at hand. What that meant for King in this particular instance was that one of his best fighting tools—Brazilian Jiu Jitsu—was off the table to be used as a weapon. As he continued to circle to Ryker's left, he took one last glance at the two trucks shining their head-lights behind Ryker. The four men with Ryker had now exited the warmth of their vehicles. The reason that meant no Jiu Jitsu was because when fighting multiple assailants, the last thing a person would ever want to do is get caught at any time on the ground. Movement and agility were the keys to fighting more than one man; if someone is on the ground, they have neither.

"Circling away from my power hand?" Ryker said. "That ain't gonna help you."

Ryker was clearly dumb, and telling your opponent your strength was just plain arrogant. But King had made the mistake of being complacent in fights before; that wasn't going to happen now.

"I told you," King said. "This isn't going to go how you are expecting."

"Please stop this!" Cali had gotten back up to her feet. She was still worried about King getting hurt. She, too, was in for a surprise. "Ryker! If you hurt him, you're going to jail!"

"He already put me in jail, Cali. So shut your mouth. It's time for him to pay."

Ryker charged forward like a bull. A lot of times in this situation, King might take the time to toy with someone as cocky, yet overmatched, as Ryker. Teach him a little lesson in humility, as King himself was often taught early on in his combat training. But it was cold as hell outside, and there were four other full-grown men he was also going to have to contend with.

"No!" Cali shouted.

When Ryker made it into striking range, he threw his bread-and-butter power right hand, and King jerked back to his right in time to miss getting hit, and simultaneously threw a left Thai kick right to Ryker's stomach. It landed with the power of a baseball bat. Ryker grunted as the air left his lungs, and dropped to his knees. As soon as King's left foot returned to the ground after the kick, he twisted his hips like a bottle cap and brought the same leg around— the top of his foot connecting with Ryker's forehead. The lights went out, and Ryker's unconscious body landed in a thud on his back.

As King squared up to the four men standing in front of

their two jacked-up pickup trucks, he glanced over at Cali and found her mouth gaped open in surprise. If the four men were surprised, they didn't show it. The first one moved in without hesitation.

"Watch out!" Cali shouted.

This guy was a round fella, wearing a double-x puffy coat and sporting lunch boxes for fists. The first of those fists came at King with about half the speed of Ryker's big punch. This guy was no Golden Gloves champion. King weaved left and tripped the big guy. He went down like a boulder off a cliff. King took two quick steps to round himself to the man's head and soccer kicked him into unconsciousness.

Unlike the movies, the rest of the men didn't line up one by one ready to get taken out. The next two came at him at the same time, but they weren't what King was worried about. It was the last man who moved around to the bed of his truck that got his attention. If he was going for a bat, or a knife, or even a tire iron, King would be okay. But if it was a gun, things were going to go sideways.

13

Moscow, Russia, 8:30 p.m.

Sam lay motionless on the ground. The cold was starting to really work its way in from the ground below her. The commotion of the gunmen chasing the man who'd picked up the briefcase had moved about twenty yards and several cars in the parking lot away. She tried to look for them without moving her head, but couldn't see them. The shooting had just stopped, so they must have run him down. The next thing they were going to do was open the briefcase. As soon as they found it was empty, they were going to double back for her. This was probably her only chance to get away.

She glanced around once more, but there were too many car tires in her line of sight to tell if the men were coming back. She was just going to have to move and hope. Sam pushed up to her knees but had no time to raise her gun before the shadowy figure in front of her kicked her in the chest, knocking her onto her back. The lights from the building showed a man pointing a gun at her. Dead to rights.

"Where are the vials?" The man spoke with a thick Russian accent.

Sam sat up. "They're in my pocket. You can have them. Just please don't kill me."

"Who sent you?" the man said.

Sam had to think fast. "No one. I am just a hired gun for Veronika. But I couldn't protect her. She's . . ." Sam trailed off for effect. She thought of all the things she could have told the man, but acting as extra security for Veronika left her the least exposed.

"Hand over vials. Slowly."

As Sam rose to her feet, she looked past the man holding the gun on her and saw the two others in the distance, just beginning to turn her way. If she wanted to make it out of there alive, now was her chance. And she had to make a sacrifice.

Sam pulled the two vials from her front pocket.

"Slow," the man reiterated.

Sam did exactly as he asked. She moved in slow motion as she extended the vials toward him. His eyes were fixed on them, not her. She located her gun just under the car on her right. The man began to reach for the vials, and that's when Sam tossed them off to her left.

As the two glass vials dropped toward the concrete, Sam fired a right kick that smacked the man's hand hard enough to dislodge the gun. The man staggered back in confusion. He was too worried about the vials breaking on the pavement to recover fast enough to defend himself. Sam stepped forward and push-kicked him in the stomach as hard as she could. It moved him back about three feet. She hoped it was enough.

As soon as her foot planted after the kick, she dove under the car, sliding her hand over the grip on her Glock. The man recovered, started forward, but it was too late. Sam squeezed the trigger twice, and down he went.

A man shouted in Russian out in front of her. Sam popped up from behind the car, and the two men were running right for her—completely exposed. She squeezed the trigger until the slide locked back. Fortunately, she was the only one left standing. Sacrificing the vials was the only way she would have been able to survive that encounter. It was exactly why she gave Zhanna the other two. And it had paid off.

Sam tucked her gun in her coat pocket, walked over to the man's gun she'd dislodged, and pocketed it as well. Then she went back to the man in uniform. He was one of the three men in uniform who had run at her from inside the hangar. She rummaged through his pockets but found only a set of keys. Her early read on the men in uniform was that they were there to make sure Veronika got the vials safely. She was thinking they were government men sent to escort her to wherever Veronika was going with the vials. When they heard the commotion Sam had created inside the hangar, they'd gone in to help.

The real question mark was the two men in suits who'd also been waiting there. They were obviously not affiliated with the military men, therefore the reason they were dead. But when one of them had shouted earlier, in Chinese, it seemed to sync with the image of the men getting off the jet with the vials. It was all so strange. Russians, Chinese, vials they were willing to die for. There was a lot to put together, and it was beginning to feel like more of a Rubik's Cube.

Sam stayed low and weaved her way around the cars to see if she could find some identification on one of those men. First, she stopped at the man she'd shot first who had been running behind the man who picked up the briefcase a moment ago and shot Sam in the shoulder. The light fixed to the building was shining on his body like a spotlight. His pockets were all empty. Whoever these suited men were, they were professionals. They probably kept their credentials locked in the glove box of their vehicle. And she had to find this vehicle before she left. She desperately needed to know who these men were. It would be key in finding out just who the players were in all of this madness about a virus.

SHE HAD SO MANY QUESTIONS, but she had to move on.

She bypassed the other two uniformed men she had shot, and went directly over to the man they'd killed for the briefcase. When she rolled the dead man over, her shoulder reminded her that there was a bullet there. Her adrenaline must have been wearing off. She could feel the wet blood running cold down her arm. She went through the man's pockets. The only thing she found was another set of keys. Maybe this was how she could get some important information.

Her head shot up and her eyes searched the road when she heard the rumbling of an engine. There were two sets of headlights moving along the road, and they were moving fast. They were definitely coming for her. She hit the lock button on the keypad a couple of times, and a horn honked.

She ran in the direction of the sound. Unfortunately, it was also in the direction of the vehicles whose tires were squealing as they turned into the airport entrance and busted through the wood plank board barrier.

She hit the lock button again, and this time when she heard the honk, she saw the caution lights flash. It was an SUV about thirty yards in front of her. The two racing vehicles were already in the parking lot. There was no time to escape with the car before they were on her, so before the vehicles turned down her lane, she bolted over to the row of cars the SUV was parked in and ducked behind the first car there. The two vehicles knew exactly where they were going. They roared past her, heading right for the hangar where the briefcase deal had gone sour. Sam scurried behind the row of cars and moved over to the driver's side of the dead men's SUV. She unlocked the door, and just as she was sliding inside, she heard sirens in the distance.

The walls were closing in.

14

BARROW, ALASKA, 9:32 A.M.

THE TWO MEN were on top of King before he could see what
the last man standing in their group was pulling out of the
back of the truck. King ducked a wild right hand thrown by
the first man and pushed him down to the ground. His
momentum did most of the work. He then managed to get
his forearms up in front of his face to block the punch
thrown by the second man. The guy followed it with a kick,
which King checked by raising his leg. The shin-to-shin
contact was too much for Ryker's crony, and he hopped off
in pain. King's Muay Thai training had deadened the nerves
in his own shin, so now he could focus on the man coming
from the back of the truck. Through a squinted eye he was
happy to see the glint of a metal baseball bat instead of a
shotgun.

The extra time he took to discern the man's weapon of
choice took too long. The first man he'd pushed to the

ground was quicker than King expected, and he jumped on King's back. He tried to put King in a choke hold, but he was sloppy. King slid his right hand through the small gap between the man's arm and his own neck, grabbed his forearm while reaching back with his other hand and wrapping it around the back of the man's head. King arched forward as he pulled the man on his back and slung him onto the ground in front of him.

"Stop! I'm calling the police!"

Both King and the man with the baseball bat shouted, "No!" at the same time. Cali looked at King like he had three heads.

"They're trying to kill you!"

King saw her point, but the last thing he wanted was more law enforcement.

"Please," King said. "Just let me handle this."

The man with the bat laughed as his buddy King had just shucked from his back rose to his feet. "Yeah, just let him handle it." The man spit what King assumed was tobacco on the ground.

Cali just stood there with her phone in her hand, unsure of what to do or say next. King could hear a groan from beside him. Ryker was regaining consciousness, and the man with the hurt shin had finally stopped hopping in pain. King needed to move to end this now or he was going to have a problem.

King stepped forward and chopped the man in the throat who had climbed his back. As he bent over in pain, King grabbed him by the shoulders and moved him in the way of the baseball bat being swung his way by the second man. The bat bounced off the man's back he was holding. King dropped him and rushed the man with the bat before he could pull back for another swing. He lifted up from under the man's arms and threw him into the grill of one of the trucks.

"Behind you!" Cali shouted.

King whipped around and weaved out of the way of a haymaker from Hopping Man, then twisted his hips and landed a left hook that popped his jaw. He turned back to the man with the bat and stepped on his arm, pinning the bat against the ground. He glanced over his shoulder and back-climber guy was on his way. King jerked the bat free, spun out of the way of another wide punch as he swung left-handed, hitting him in the stomach with the bat.

By this time, Ryker had made it to his feet. King was lucky. He just so happened to be looking Ryker's way when he was reaching for the small of his back. There is only one thing ever hidden there. King knew a gun was coming out.

"Ryker! No!" Cali shouted.

But King had already launched the bat. It flew end over end and struck Ryker in the leg. It was by no means a destructive blow, but it was enough to give King the chance to chase behind the bat and dive into Ryker as he tried to dodge the bat and pull the gun at the same time. The gun went off as King landed on top of him. He wasted no time delivering an elbow to Ryker's jaw. Once again, Ryker was out. That's when he heard Cali scream.

King jumped up off Ryker, fearing the worst, that Cali had been hit by the stray bullet. Instead, she was looking at the round man whom King had kicked unconscious. He was on his knees, clutching at his neck. There was just enough light to see the blood spraying from it.

Cali screamed again.

"Call an ambulance!" King shouted to her.

He removed his coat and ran over to the man who was gasping for air. He wrapped his coat around the man's neck, tied the arms of the coat, and pulled it as tight as he could. But once King was on top of him, he could tell it was no use. He'd seen enough wounds like this to know this man was going to die.

"There's no time for the ambulance," King shouted to the men who were trying to recover. "You have to drive him, fast, or he's going to die!"

There was no animosity left in the men. Instead, two of them rushed over to the big man and hoisted him up under his arms. King lifted his legs, and they carried him over to the back of the truck. The other man was trying to get Ryker up off the ground. King rushed over and helped the man lift him.

"This is a crime scene now, Xavier," Cali said. "You can't move him. I have to call the sheriff. Ryker just shot that guy."

"No he didn't!" the man lifting Ryker said. Then he looked King in the eye. "I saw you shoot Ronnie. Didn't you see it, Rick?" he said to the man who'd had the bat.

"Sure as hell did! Now let's go!"

King dropped Ryker. He didn't have time to argue. He couldn't be involved either way. He just needed to go.

"Bullshit! I saw the whole thing!" Cali shouted.

Rick climbed into his truck. "Yeah? You sure about that?"

"I'm damn sure!"

The other men had come to help get Ryker into the truck.

The guy who'd climbed on King's back earlier stopped

and took a long look at Cali. "We know where to find you. Just remember that, sweetheart."

King's instinct was to change the man's mind on that statement with a violent amount of force. But the ambulance Cali called was crying in the distance, and the truck with the man with the hole in his neck was already backing up. The sheriff would hear the ambulance call on the wire. There wasn't much that happened in Barrow, so he'd be all over this.

"You just try me, you redneck!" Cali said.

King walked over and took her by the waist. Through all that was happening, he could feel his arms going numb from the cold. He needed to get inside and get the only other coat he'd brought; then he needed to get the hell out of there. He'd just completely blown everything he was in Alaska for. The next few steps were going to be all about saving what little bit of this mission he could.

With the virologist actually there, in Barrow, under an alias—working under lockdown and top secret conditions —King knew he couldn't just leave things as they were. There was far too much at stake. He was going to have to call in a favor, but the new director of the CIA wasn't going to like it.

15

When the SUVs stopped at the hangar, four men jumped out. Sam watched intently from the SUV she'd commandeered from the dead man a few moments ago. She didn't want to start the engine for fear of revealing her location to the men by the hangar. However, the sirens she heard were getting louder, and it was happening fast. Her next thought was which route to take. If she went out the exit, she would almost certainly pass the police, or military, or whatever was heading her way. If she took Zhanna's route through the fence, it would be clear that she was someone trying to flee the situation and would probably get the attention of everyone.

Sam watched as the men in suits split up under the lights fixed to the hangar. Two went inside the hangar, and two went to check out the dead bodies left lying in the parking lot. This was the best chance she was going to get.

73

She started the SUV, put it in drive, and eased out of the parking space. She didn't turn on the SUV's lights just yet. She was hoping the drivers in the vehicles by the hangar would be distracted by the bodies lying in front of them. As soon as she made it to the lane that led to the exit, she flipped on the headlights. The last thing she wanted was for the police rounding the corner to see an SUV driving without its lights. They would be after her for sure.

As she rolled toward the entrance, she pulled out her phone and dialed Zhanna. As it rang, off to her right out on the road the flashing lights became visible. Her stomach turned. She was in a terrible position. Not only had she been shot, but in order to escape, she had to lose the only evidence she had of what the meeting was about. And to make things worse, Zhanna's phone rang all the way to voice mail. Not a good sign.

Sam approached the exit. As she rolled through the gate and turned on her left turn signal, to go in the direction Zhanna had driven, she had to stop and wait for the train of four police cars to swerve around her and zoom through the private airport's entrance. As she eased out onto the road, she glanced in the rearview mirror. So far, the police cars all kept heading the same direction. Sam dialed Zhanna again. After the first ring, she noticed in her side mirror that one of the police cars she'd passed had just broken off from the other three. Its headlights whipped around the opposite direction, and Sam immediately laid on the gas pedal.

They were coming after her.

As the call to Zhanna kept ringing, Sam took the first right turn she came upon. It was dark. The private airport was outside the city in a rural area. If she didn't get some distance between her and the police car circling back for her, being isolated out there would make it much harder for her to get away. A city would offer traffic she could blend into, get lost in. The only thing around her now was the occasional home and darkness.

The call went to a generic voice mail, and Sam made another right turn. Now she was worried. She of course cared about the safety of Zhanna, but if someone found her and took the only vials left from the briefcase, millions of people's lives could be in danger. Sam sped down an empty road. She had no idea where she was going. A sick feeling washed over her. Her mind began thinking the worst. That Zhanna was in trouble, that their only lead on the potential deadly virus was dead, and she had no plan as to what might be her next move.

Her phone began to ring.

Hope returned when she saw the number. The same number she'd been calling to reach Zhanna.

"Zhanna, thank God. Where are—"

"You are British?" A man's voice with a thick Russian accent interrupted Sam's momentary relief.

Her blood ran cold. They'd captured Zhanna.

Sam couldn't speak, so she just continued to drive, focusing on the man's voice and anything she may be able to hear in the background. Her mind was racing. Was Zhanna hurt? Dead? Does this man have the vials? If so, what can she do now without any evidence from the brief-case? Before the man spoke again, the image of the tail number on the plane that the man with the briefcase of vials flew in on popped in her head: *Z450XY*. If she couldn't find Zhanna and this man, the tail number was her only lead.

"Who do you work for?" the man asked.

Sam put the call on speaker and switched to the text message app in her phone. She pulled up Dbie Johnson's contact, Alexander King's resident techie. She typed out a message as the man breathed into the phone: *Run down the tail number of this private plane. Z450XY. I need to know who owns it and where it comes from. Before you do that, track down this phone's location immediately. 341-555-2943. Life or death.*

Dbie instantly messaged back: *On it.*

Sam had given her Zhanna's number in hopes she could find its location.

"Don't feel like talking?" the man said. "No problem."

"Wait!" Sam said. She had to make the call last as long as she could so Dbie could get a location. And she also wanted to probe and see if she could get anything from this man. "I have the other two vials." She had no choice but to push all her chips into the pot.

"So this woman is important to you," the man said through what sounded like a grin.

"She is. Please don't hurt her."

As Sam glanced down at her phone to check and see if Dbie had messaged, flashing blue lights caught her eye in the rearview mirror. Sam had become so engrossed in the phone call and messaging Dbie that she'd neglected to make a few more turns to help her lose the police. She stomped on the brakes and took a quick left, sped up, and squealed the tires for another right. She floored it again, but she had no idea where she was going.

"Ul. Lesnaya d. 5, kv. 176," the man gave an address. "Six in morning. No vials? No woman."

The man ended the call.

Sam spotted an underpass up ahead. She must be near the highway. The police would find her if she went that way, so instead, she drove into the trees in the field beside her, shut off the lights, and killed the engine. She hoped the police wouldn't see her and would drive on by, but if they didn't, she had a backup plan.

Sam received a message from Dbie. She didn't have to open the phone to know what it said. The man had ended the call and busted the phone before Dbie could find the phone's location.

Sam checked her rearview. After a few more seconds, the police car went driving by. But before she could breathe a sigh of relief, she heard tires squalling on pavement. The police had seen her. She didn't want to have to kill an innocent police officer, but she couldn't be taken in.

All she could do was hope her backup plan would work.

16

BARROW, ALASKA, 9:35 A.M.

KING THREW ON HIS COAT, grabbed his Glock, phone, and knife, all while Cali was taking a shot of Canadian whiskey in the kitchen.

"Not sure that's going to help," King said as he walked in from the bedroom.

"Can't hurt."

"Just how well do you know those guys?"

"Better than I know you, obviously," she said as she set down the bottle.

"We don't have time for this. Or I don't. It's up to you what you want to do next."

"What the hell are you going to do? There is nowhere to hide here. You do understand that, right?"

"That's why I'm asking how well you know them. Will they try to hurt you to keep you from telling the sheriff you saw Ryker shoot the big guy and not me?"

Her pause was enough to tell him what he needed to know. If she was right, and there really was nowhere to hide, King was going to need help.

"Call the police," he said.

She looked at him like he'd asked for a lethal injection. "You can't be serious."

"You called him Josiah last night, so you obviously know him. Call him and tell him to come here."

"Guaranteed he's already on his way here. And yes, I know him, X, but you're the new guy in town. He's not going to stand by you."

"But will he stand by you? He seemed awfully fond of you."

"I-I don't know."

"It doesn't matter. Will you please just call him so he doesn't try to barge in with a gun? This mess with Ryker is the least of my worries."

"I assure you it isn't," Cali's hands were on her hips. "He thinks he runs this town. He'll come after you. He and even more of his redneck crew. Josiah won't be able to stop him. That's just the way it is here. He only put Ryker in jail last night as a favor to Ryker. Those Russian guys are the only people here more dangerous than Ryker."

"You don't understand." King searched the drawer for a backup beanie hat. "Just call the sheriff and everything will make sense."

"Okay. But I can't help you once Josiah gets here."

King looked up at her. "How could you help me if I left before then? You said there was nowhere to hide."

"There isn't . . . *here*. But my dad has a plane. I can get you out of here before tonight."

Before King could ask for more details, they heard a car pull up and then a voice coming out of a bullhorn.

"No need to call the sheriff," Cali said as she walked toward the door.

King pulled his phone and dialed Robert Lucas. He answered in one ring but didn't immediately speak.

"X2112," King said. It was his verification code for the director of the CIA to be assured it was him.

"X? Speak freely. Everything all right?"

"I wouldn't be calling if it was."

Cali stepped outside into the cold to head off the sheriff.

"That's what I was afraid of. How bad is it?"

"It's a long story. I have to blow my cover, but only to the sheriff in town."

"No way, X. Get on the next plane out of there. We'll send someone else."

"There's no time. Our target is here. I have to follow up."

That brought a long sigh. King knew his proposal would be met with pushback.

"Let me make a couple of calls, and I'll talk to the sheriff."

"No time for that either," King said. "He's here to take me to jail, and I have to go to work tonight. I'm going to find out what they're hiding here."

King knew that would do the trick. While the absolute last thing Director Lucas would want to happen would be for an agent to let people know who they were actually working for, there was one thing worse than that: a virus spreading and killing thousands or more when it could have been stopped.

Cali and Josiah walked through the door and shut it behind them. Josiah was holding handcuffs.

"I'm going to need you to talk to the sheriff right now, 'cause he just walked in."

"Put the phone down," Josiah said to King. "You're under arrest."

"I told you, they came after *him*, Josiah," Cali pleaded. "You have to listen to me."

"Right now I have to take him in. We can sort this whole mess out down at the station."

"I'm not going to resist, sheriff," King said as he put up his hands. Then he extended the phone toward him. "But can you please take this call first?"

The sheriff walked over and took the phone. Probably out of sheer curiosity. What potential prisoner would ever ask the sheriff to talk to someone on the phone?

Josiah took the phone but spoke to King. "What the hell is this? Your mommy to plead with me to let you go?"

"It's the director of the CIA."

Josiah laughed, and Cali's jaw nearly hit the floor.

"Just when you think you've heard it all," Josiah said as he put the phone to his ear. "This is the sheriff."

King looked at Cali. He wasn't sure what the confused expression on her face meant, but it seemed to be turning into a more knowing one the longer she looked at him. Like the puzzle pieces were coming together. New guy in town in abnormally good shape, admittedly former military, fighting skills enough to take down four men. King was sure that was what she was computing.

"Yeah, and I'm Santa-fucking-Claus, Mr. CIA Director."

Apparently Director Lucas hadn't been very convincing.

Josiah ended the call and laid the phone down on the table. "Turn around and put your hands behind your back, Mr. CIA."

King, like Cali, was doing some computing of his own. If he took down the sheriff and avoided being taken into custody, was there any way he could still accomplish what he came to Barrow to do? No. His only chance was to go to work that night at Volkov Mining like nothing had ever happened, and make his way into the secure room where Dmitry Kuznetsov was doing his secret work. That would be impossible if the entire police force was after him, no matter how small that force might be. Instead, he had to trust that before it was time for his shift at work, Director Lucas would figure out a way to convince Josiah to let King go free.

King had a feeling that wouldn't be much of a problem, considering the president of the United States himself had personally put King on the job.

17

THE RUSSIAN POLICE car pulled in behind Sam's SUV that was tucked in a grouping of trees just before the on-ramp to the freeway. As he was shouting something in Russian through his vehicle's loud speaker, Sam removed her jacket. In the blinking blue lights, she could see that the sleeve of her white turtleneck shirt was covered in blood from her shoulder down. This would help sell her backup plan.

Sam then rested her head against the steering wheel, and looked as passed out as she possibly could. The policeman had stopped shouting through the speaker system, and the next thing she heard was a door slam. He was coming for her. She took a few deep breaths to steady herself. If she could catch the officer off guard, she wouldn't have to kill him. That said, her Glock was tucked between the seat and the console beside her, just in case.

The policeman shouted something in Russian, took a

quick pause, then shouted again. He was right outside her door. He was probably terrified at who might come out shooting at him, so he was going to be on high alert. Sam knew she would have to be fast. All the policeman was working off of was that this SUV was fleeing the scene of a multiple homicide. His trigger finger would be itchy. Sam also knew he'd already called for backup. She just prayed he wasn't going to wait for it to arrive. Because if he didn't open the door to find her *incapacitated*, she was going to have to shoot him and leave. It was the last resort.

The policeman shouted again. Inside her head Sam pleaded with him to be a hero. Then she heard him bang on the window beside her. He'd gotten close enough to see her. He was going to open the door. Sam readied herself.

The car door flung open, and cold air rushed in as the policeman shouted frantically. Sam didn't move. By now he'd noticed the blood in the beam of his flashlight. He shouted again. She was still as a statue. The policeman didn't put his gun away; instead, he moved over to her and actually poked her near the wound in her shoulder with it. A bolt of pain shot down Sam's arm, but she didn't move.

The policeman shouted one last time; then Sam heard his tone change when his radio squawked. He was letting his fellow officers know that he had the suspect in custody. He spoke in Russian, but the fear and tension had left his voice, so Sam knew that he thought it was over. She knew she had him.

The policeman released the button on his radio, and Sam heard the snap on his holster engage. As soon as he wrapped his hand around her dangling left wrist and pulled her into an upright position, Sam shot her right hand directly into his throat. The man staggered back in shock as he gasped for breath. As he fumbled for his gun, Sam slid off the seat and kicked him in the groin. He doubled over onto his knees. Sam delivered a knockout kick to his forehead, and the man collapsed to the ground. He would have a hell of a headache in the morning, but at least he would be alive.

Sam didn't bother taking his radio. She knew his counterparts were already on their way. That and the sirens that filled the quiet night in the distance reiterated that fact. She did, however, relieve him of his weapon, because her magazine was almost empty. She reached inside the truck and threw her coat back on. At this point her shoulder was screaming. She was going to have to find someone who could remove the bullet and patch her up. But first, she had to get somewhere safe.

Sam jumped back in the SUV, threw it into reverse and smashed into the front of the police car, giving her enough room to turn in front of the trees. As she merged onto the freeway, her first call was to Director Lucas. Normally there would be a handler for an agent in the field instead of the head of the CIA, but because her and Alexander King's involvement were only known by Director Lucas and the president of the United States, there was no one else to reach out to.

Director Lucas answered. "Sam, I can't talk right now, X is in trouble."

With all that had transpired in the last two hours, it hadn't occurred to her to check on King. She checked the time and realized she was supposed to have messaged him, but he was supposed to be in bed. Her stomach tied in a knot.

"X? He's supposed to be sleeping off night shift. Is he all right?"

"He's fine, but the mission is not."

Sam already knew the mission wasn't fine, hence all the dead bodies at the hangar. She was just glad to hear X was okay.

"But I've got to go, Sam. They are taking him to jail."

A hundred things ran through her mind. She knew Alexander King better than anyone. He was the very best at what he did with one small exception: he thinks he can save everyone. Sam had no idea what the trouble was with King, but she would have bet her life on it that the trouble he was in was because he was trying to help someone he should never have been involved with. And like she told the president at the speakeasy in Washington the night he gave X this critical mission, she would bet it all that it had to do with a woman. But at least he wasn't hurt.

"Sam? I guess I should have asked if you are okay."

Sam didn't need Director Lucas right now. She knew one of the other agents in place whom the CIA had embedded in Moscow. He would be able to help her with a doctor—and with the little meeting she had scheduled the next morning. She just needed his phone number.

"I'm fine. Worry about X. I just need Patrick O'Connor's contact information."

"I'll send it shortly," Director Lucas said. "Anything else?"

"Yeah, have X call me, would you?"

"Will do. I'll check back with you shortly."

Sam dialed Dbie Johnson once again. Two years ago she didn't even know Dbie; now she didn't know what she would do without her. Having someone only X and Sam knew about was turning out to be a very helpful thing.

Especially when Dbie answered the phone and already had information about the private plane that had flown into Moscow carrying vials filled with a mysterious liquid that a lot of people were finding extremely important. Including the man holding Zhanna hostage.

18

"Josiah, you're making a mistake," Cali said as Josiah wrapped the handcuffs around King's wrists. "CIA or not, he didn't do anything wrong."

Josiah clicked the last cuff in place, then put his hands on his hips. "Yeah? Well, I have a man bleeding out from a gunshot wound over at the hospital, and four people say it was CIA here that pulled the trigger."

"And I'm telling you it wasn't. It wasn't even his gun!"

"Well, if that's the case, Xavier here will have nothing to worry about." The tall, dark-haired sheriff turned to King. "Come on now. Don't make this difficult for me, or I'll make it that way for you."

King didn't have a choice but to go without incident. At that point, fighting back would only make things worse. He gave Josiah a nod.

"Now my deputy is going to search the place. Anything I

need to know about before she does? Judge might be lenient if you cooperate."

King looked him in the eye. "There's a bottle of Canadian whiskey in the cabinet. But I had nothing to do with that either."

Cali laughed.

Josiah did not. "You think this is funny? You're the new guy here, and I've got Barrow citizens at the hospital because of you."

Now King was starting to get upset. He was from a small town, so he knew how the politics in such a place worked, but this was beginning to go beyond that. "In case you haven't noticed sheriff, those boys came to me. I didn't seek them out. The last thing I wanted was to find trouble."

"Well, whether you found it or it found you, it's here."

Josiah nudged King toward the door.

"You can't be serious, Josiah," Cali said. "I'm an eyewitness who you know personally, and I'm telling you they attacked him, and it was Ryker who accidentally shot his own friend after he pulled his gun on Xavier. Ryker is the man you should be taking to jail!"

Josiah stopped. "He's probably going to jail, too, but I will not have this shit going on in my town." Josiah looked back at King. "I suggest you save the talking for your lawyer. He's the only person who can really help you now."

King didn't say a word. Just when Josiah pulled him forward, Josiah's radio beeped. He stopped to respond. "Go ahead, Elaine."

"Sheriff, I don't really know how to say this . . ."

King knew immediately what was about to happen. He wasn't going to jail.

"What is it, Elaine? Spit it out."

"Um . . . well . . . you have a phone call."

"You know what's going on out here, Elaine, and you're bothering me about a phone call? Take a message."

"Sir, it's . . . it's someone claiming to be calling on behalf of the president of the United States." Elaine stopped talking long enough to laugh out loud. "Said it was a matter of national security. I'm sorry to bother you, but I figured with the shit you're dealing with, you could use a laugh."

Josiah looked back at King. He knew it wasn't a prank. Not after hanging up on someone claiming to be the director of the CIA. "This shit for real?"

The time for messing around was over. King needed to get moving on what he came to Alaska to do. This extracurricular bullshit had to stop, and he needed to pivot. He had an idea that he hoped might actually benefit him. "It's for real. And I need your help."

Josiah took out the keys to the handcuffs as he pressed his radio. "Have them call my cell phone."

Elaine came back with a laugh. "Okay, boss. See you when you get back to the station."

"No, Elaine. Have them call my cell phone, and tell no one the call came in."

"Oh, okay. Sending them to your cell."

"Elaine?"

"Yeah?"

"Don't tell anyone, or you're fired."

Josiah nodded to King. King had made the right play asking for help. It was already paying off. Josiah stuck the key in the handcuffs and released them.

"Holy shit," Cali said. "I mean, the way you handled yourself out there, that was crazy, but CIA? What the hell could be going on here in this town to warrant bringing you here undercover?"

"The Russians," Josiah spoke up. Then he looked at King. "Tell me I'm wrong."

"You understand I can't say a whole lot."

Cali walked over beside Josiah, and they both waited with bated breath.

"What I can tell you is that millions of American lives are at stake. It's that serious. And I have a lead." King looked at Josiah. "I just might need you to help make sure I can run it down."

Before Josiah could answer, his cell phone rang.

"You know you have got to put that on speaker, right?" Cali said.

"This really gonna be President Gibbons?"

"It is," King said.

Josiah held out his phone, hit speaker—much to Cali's delight—and answered the call. "This is Sheriff Lee."

"Sheriff, please hold for the president."

Cali held her hand over her open mouth. Josiah just stared blankly at his phone.

"Sheriff Lee?" a man's voice asked.

"Yes. Yes, sir."

"This is President Gibbons. I hear you have one of my finest agents there with you. That correct?"

"That's what he tells me, sir."

"Can I speak with him?"

"I'm here, Mr. President," King said. "Sorry to have to bother you like this, but as you know, things don't always go according to plan."

Just a few months ago, before the election, King had saved the president and his wife from a rogue CIA agent. It's the reason King didn't really feel bad about the president having to make a phone call.

"I know that all too well," the president said. "You all right?"

"I am now, sir."

"Sheriff?"

"Yes, Mr. President?"

"I probably don't have to tell you that because you're getting a call from me, it means something dead serious is going on. I'll leave it up to my agent to fill you in how he sees fit, but you'd be doing your country, and me, a great favor if you could lend him your services. The safety of our citizens depends on it."

"I'll do whatever is needed, sir. I can assure you of that."

"That's great. And it won't go unnoticed. Now you need to understand that this call never happened. And you need to know that the man standing beside you, after he leaves Barrow, Alaska, was only ever Xavier, the security guard at Volkov Mining from out of town who just couldn't handle the cold."

"That last part might actually be true," King interjected.

"I imagine so, X. Sheriff, are we on the same page?"

"Yes, sir. Absolutely."

"Fine. Thank you for your help. X, try to stay out of trouble, would you?"

"No sir. I think I'm about to find a whole lot more of it."

"Oorah. Contact Director Lucas when you get a minute. And good luck."

"Thanks for the call, sir," King said.

The call ended.

"Wow," Cali spoke first.

"Listen," King said, finding both Cali's and Josiah's eyes.

"This is for real. You need to understand that it's not just life and death, it's a lot of lives, and possibly a whole lot of deaths."

"What's going on?" Josiah said.

"I won't say much, but remember how fast the coronavirus swept the country, and the globe?"

Both Cali's and Josiah's faces shifted from curious to concerned. It felt odd for King to be sharing this kind of information; it was the first time since he'd joined the military that he had conveyed details about a mission to civilians while he was in the middle of it. But at that point, he had no choice. He would just give as little as possible. The two of them both eventually nodded their heads.

"Well, imagine if corona had been *far* more deadly."

King watched Josiah swallow hard.

"Someone is using a virus as a weapon?" Cali asked.

"At Volkov?" Josiah finally spoke.

King headed the questions off at the pass. "All you need to know is that I have to go to work tonight as if nothing ever happened. Someone very important is here under an alias, and I have to find out tonight exactly what he's up to. Now, I can do that on my own, but it would be nice if I had someone to call in case things don't go as planned."

"Whatever you need," Josiah said.

"I'm not much help with security measures," Cali said, "but I'm here if you need me."

When Cali offered her help, King's mind flashed back to her telling him her father had a plane.

"What does your dad do?" King asked her.

"What?" The question caught Cali off guard.

"Your dad. You said he has a plane?"

"Oh, right. Transports. Mostly groceries and emergencies. As you know, there aren't a lot of flights in and out of here, so he makes needed and emergency trips along with his regular pickups and deliveries."

"And earlier you said you could get me out of here before tonight. That still an option? Even after midnight?"

"Wait a second," Josiah interrupted, then shot a look at Cali. "You were offering to help him escape?"

Cali smiled. "You can't escape if you didn't do anything. I was just going to help him leave if he was wrongfully accused. And if you remember correctly, that's exactly what you were here doing."

"I wasn't accusing—"

"Can we focus here?" King jumped in. "Some pretty big stuff going on . . . remember? The president just called you and such?"

They both apologized, and Cali picked up where King had left off. "Yes to your question. If you need to get out of here, anytime, you can."

"Your dad would be available?" King asked.

"Doesn't need to be," Josiah answered for her. "Cali's a pilot. She'll fly you."

King raised his eyebrow and smirked like he was impressed. Because he was. He liked the woman he was involved with to have layers. And Cali was quickly becoming a tall cake's worth.

"Sexy, right?" Josiah said.

Cali didn't blush. She just held out her arms and shrugged.

Sexy was a good word for her. She was that in every way.

King's phone began to ring. And as if Sam could somehow sense King was starting to feel something for a woman who would only cause him problems, she was calling to snap him back to reality.

"Good timing, Sam," King answered. "You missed your check-in, by the way."

"Yeah? Well, some of us are working a mission instead of working a woman."

It was as if she had full camera access to him at all times. How the hell could she—

"Let me guess, how the hell could I know about that already, right?"

She was a sorceress.

Sam continued. "Well, when I called Director Lucas for the agent-in-place's number so I could get help taking this bullet out of my shoulder, he put me on hold to bail you out of jail."

"Bullet?!" King nearly shouted. "Sam, are you—"

"I'm fine. Relax. But we need to talk. Someone's been flying samples of something out of Barrow, Alaska."

"Samples? What are you talking about?"

"Not sure yet, but they were important enough to get me caught in a bloody war over them at a hangar in Moscow. If Zhanna hadn't been there, you and I wouldn't be having this conversation."

"Zhanna? What the hell was she doing there?" This thing was getting more and more tangled by the minute.

"I'm really not sure."

"You can't just ask her?'

"No brainiac, I can't just ask her," Sam snapped at him. "She's being held hostage. She had the only two samples left unbroken when they took her."

"Hostage?" King looked over at Cali. "I'm leaving right now, Sam. I'll be in Moscow by morning."

Cali nodded as if she were ready to help.

"Xander, no you won't. There is no room for your '*save everyone*' mentality right now. I'm on it. Trust me. I'll do everything I can to get her back. We need you there right now. You have got to find out what they are flying out of there, and why. And it needs to be tonight."

King looked down and realized he was clenching his fist. He took a deep breath and steadied himself. Sam was right. He was right where he needed to be. And now that the nonsense with the locals was over, he could focus his full attention back on the task at hand.

"I'm on it. You sure you're all right?" King said.

"I'm fine. Just keep me updated. It's getting late here. By the time you get to your shift tonight, I should have Zhanna back. Then we'll just need some answers. They could be ready to spread this thing, Xander. I think we are right there."

"Just focus on getting Zhanna. And keep me updated, Sam. No more missing check-ins."

"And no more playing hero to whatever her name is and her local thugs."

"I hear you."

"I'm sure you do, X. But it isn't your hearing I'm worried about. It's your libido."

"Love you too, Sam."

Sam ended the call. King looked at Cali. "Tell me more about what it is exactly that your father transports."

19

JOSIAH HAD TO LEAVE KING'S PLACE TO GO SORT OUT WHAT had happened out front just about a half hour ago. King had a moment to catch his breath. His shift didn't start for hours, though he didn't think he could possibly wait that long to make a move. Not with all that was going on in Moscow. King and Cali reheated their coffee and sat back down at the table.

"Well, I gotta say," Cali said, pausing to take a sip of her coffee, "that went in a direction I didn't see it going."

"Yeah, I should still be asleep."

"Sorry I spoiled your plans in Barrow there, sport."

"They aren't spoiled yet, but I imagine this isn't the first time you derailed a man's plans."

She smiled. "I suppose not." Cali tucked her hair back behind her ear. Though she wasn't a soft woman, her features were. Her golden skin looked smooth as silk, and the smile she flashed was wide and bright. "I know you're not supposed to talk about it, but what's it like being an undercover agent? Don't you get lonely?"

King set his mug on the table and let out a sigh. "I didn't used to get lonely. It wasn't always just me. Not too long ago I had a team and we were always together."

"That woman on the phone?"

"Yeah. She's like my sister. My good friend and a few other folks who became close all ran with me."

"What happened?"

"Long story."

"I'm sorry." She sat forward in her seat and placed her hand over King's. "I know it's not the same, but I can sort of relate. When my dad moved us here, I left my *team* too. We moved several times in California, but nothing like this. When you move to a place like this, nothing can prepare you for it."

"No kidding?" He gave her a smile. "Why did you move with your father? It isn't like you're a teenager without a life."

"When Mom died, he was lost. And I was always a daddy's girl, so I did what I'd always done and tagged along. Things weren't going how I'd hoped at home anyway, so I figured a change would be good."

"I get it," he said. "You're right, it isn't the same, but I can relate too."

They were quiet for a moment. It seemed the two of them, though not much alike, had several things they found in common. In the quiet moment King worried about Sam and Zhanna. Somehow, even though he was always in the middle of shit, he always found himself too far away to help someone on his team. And Zhanna popping up out of nowhere was the strangest thing. Especially now that she was being held hostage.

"Where'd you go?" Cali broke the silence. She released his hand and continued to sip her coffee.

"Worried about my friends."

"You're not used to *not* being able to save someone, are you?"

"Guess not." King drank from his mug.

"Listen, I can go if you need time to think, or strategize. I don't want to be in the way."

King sat back and ran his fingers through his hair. "You're fine. Really. It's nice to have some company. I do want to hear more about your father's operation, though, if you don't mind."

"Sure. It's not all that interesting, though."

"My shift doesn't start for hours."

Cali laughed. "Okay, well, as you know, there are no roads connecting this town to civilization, so we rely on planes to get supplies in and out. Dad and his friend are the only private source for doing so. The government pays them to carry mail and other supplies, and they are available for emergencies."

"What type of supplies? Ever anything from Volkov?"

"You trying to imply something," she asked protectively.

"No. I just need to know what's happening here. And just because your father flew things for Volkov, that wouldn't mean he is involved."

"I'm not sure if *things* from Volkov Mining have been flown or not, but I know for sure that people have."

Some flags flew up for King. "Makes sense. Where does your dad usually fly to?"

"Mostly just the cities directly surrounding us, but once a week, if there is enough demand, they fly all the way to

Anchorage. Been more demand lately with the uptick in Russians working at Volkov. They pay extra, so Dad doesn't ask any questions. After meeting you, I'm thinking maybe he should start. Not really sure why they don't just use the commercial planes that go there. Guess that's why you're here."

King was a step beyond Cali, and he took the conversation in a different direction. "Are there a lot of flights from Anchorage to Moscow?"

"Actually, yeah. It's a long flight, but it stays busy from what I hear. Why? What's going on in that head of yours?"

"It's a dark place you wouldn't want to see." King smiled, but both of them knew it was the truth.

"I can't even imagine the things you've seen.

"Don't try."

"It can't be all bad, right?"

King thought first about the fun times he'd had with his team even during the terrible battles they'd faced. Then about the bourbon distillery he'd started years back and about his horses he'd left behind. Then he thought of Natalie Rockwell. "No, not all bad."

"So there really was a woman named Natalie?"

Cali and Natalie had more in common than just beauty. It seemed as though Cali could see right through him as Natalie had been able to do.

King nodded.

"Lucky girl."

King thought about how Natalie being tied to him had almost gotten her killed. "Not exactly."

He stood from the table. "I'm empty, you want some more coffee?"

She stood with him. "No. No more coffee." She stepped closer and took his hand.

Though it had been a long time for King since he'd seen it, he knew what the look in Cali's eyes meant. He didn't want to get involved, but he was tired of always putting work ahead of his heart. And right then, there was nothing more in the world he wanted than to be with Cali. To forget for a moment that the world was sinister. To forget he was responsible for keeping it safe. He just wanted a moment to be free.

So he kissed her.

20

"This is turning into a shitshow, Robert!" President Gibbons shouted at the CIA director.

"These are covert operations, Mr. President. Things get messy. We have the best on this, I assure you."

"I know we have the best on it. I've seen them in action. But that doesn't make it less of a mess. Shouldn't we send more people in? I want to help them!"

President Gibbons was as worried as he was angry that things weren't going well in Alaska or in Moscow. He was worried for his country but, more immediately, for his agents who had become like friends. His mentality from the Marines was "no man left behind." Sitting at a desk and waiting to see if they could pull themselves out of impossible situations wasn't sitting well. Especially with so much on the line. It wasn't a usual occurrence for the director of the CIA to be in the Oval Office so much, but when things were moving as fast and deadly as they seemed to be, things were different.

"All due respect, this isn't the Marines, sir. Our agents aren't expecting the cavalry to come and save them. They are used to working this way. We send more people in now, all we do is put them in danger."

"Danger!" The president gave a sarcastic laugh. "Like there isn't more than they can handle of that right now."

"I know. But sending them more agents isn't the way to help."

"Well, what the hell is then, Robert?"

"Information. We are processing some of the things that Sam filled us in on, like who came in on the plane with those vials."

"And what does King plan on doing with Kuznetsov?" the president asked.

"That's what you and I need to figure out."

"What are our options?"

"A couple of things really. Now that the sheriff in Barrow has been made aware of King, he might actually be able to find out where Kuznetsov is staying."

"To take him down, or what?"

"No," Director Lucas said. "We don't want to throw up any flags. If he has check-ins, we can't have him miss one. We might lose our window. I'm certain there is protocol that if he misses check-in, or doesn't show up at Volkov when he is supposed to, they'll burn his work. If this has been going on as long as I think it has, whoever is behind this will be patient enough to find a new place to get this work done. Even if it means starting over."

"So what good does it do to know where Kuznetsov is staying?" the president asked.

"We might be able to get his security badge for Volkov. Which will give us access to what they are working on."

"But then King will be burned?"

"Right. It's all or nothing. If he doesn't find something that helps us, Barrow will be no help in stopping what is being planned. It will tip them off for sure that someone is on to them. We might lose our chance of stopping it altogether."

The president took all the information in. He had faith that King would find what they needed, *if* there was something to find. He just didn't know if it was worth risking tipping their hand. They needed more information. Information that seemed to be eluding them. Someone was in charge of what Kuznetsov was doing. It looked like it could be Russia with what happened at the hangar in Moscow. But there was nothing definite there, yet. They needed some other sort of break.

Director Lucas's phone began ringing. "It's Sam."

"Isn't it getting late there? And wasn't she shot?"

"The woman is relentless."

Lucas answered the phone. "Sam, you're on speaker with the president."

"Good, we might need your connections, Mr. President."

"Whatever you need. You holding up all right?" he asked.

"Do you have any connection to Nigel Warshaw?" Sam bypassed the president's cordial question and kept it strictly business.

"Well," the president said, thinking it over, "I don't have him on speed dial, but I could get him on the phone. Why?"

"Are you aware that after his software firm made him billions, he got into the business of funding vaccinations?"

"Can't say I am. But like I said, I don't know him that well."

"Right, well, one of the labs he is heavily invested in just so happens to be the Wuhan lab in China."

"Wuhan, as in the coronavirus, Wuhan?"

"That's the one. He was also seen several months ago having lunch with Dmitry Kuznetsov after the World Health Conference in Seattle, Washington."

The president looked at Director Lucas. Lucas leaned forward, interested in what was coming next. "And?"

"*Aaand,*" Sam said, "the tail number on the private plane that the man holding the briefcase of vials walked out of is linked back to a small holding company based out of Seattle, Washington. The LLC doesn't have Nigel Warshaw's name on it, but I must say I find it all a bit odd."

President Gibbons found it all odd as well, but there were a lot of leaps being made. They couldn't go off half-cocked and start running down one of the wealthiest men in the world. "Let's be very careful about jumping to conclusions here."

"Mr. President," Sam said, "may I speak freely?"

"Please."

"We don't have time to play around. If there is a lead, we must follow it. The two men in suits who were after the briefcase were Asian. Now I'm not saying anyone is involved for sure. But I am telling you that you better find out if Warshaw is involved, or if he isn't so we can check him off the list. This virus, if that is what is being weaponized, could already be on its way to the continental United States. *Careful* is the opposite of what we should be at this moment. We have to start getting answers. And Director Lucas?"

"Yes, Sam."

"You have to let X off the leash in Barrow. Kuznetsov is there. Let X find out what else is there. Even if he has to string Kuznetsov up by his neck to get it."

"Tell us how you really feel," Director Lucas joked.

"You don't send me out into these situations to get roses and rainbows in return. Let me know what you find out about Warshaw. I have to go get a bullet removed from my shoulder."

Sam ended the call.

"I like her," the president said. "Now get me everything you know about Nigel Warshaw. Stuff only you guys can find out."

"I didn't want to talk about it in front of Sam, but we already have a running file on him."

"Then get me that file. And Sam's right, we don't have time to screw around. Let Alexander King off his leash."

21

"WELL, THAT WAS FUN," Cali said. She rolled out of bed, smacked King on the ass, and started for the bedroom door. "Call me if you need a flight outta here tonight."

A mischievous grin was the only thing she was wearing as she walked out the door.

"Leaving without your clothes?" King played back. "It's awfully cold outside."

Cali popped her head back in the door. "I was just trying to get out of here before you saw through my act."

"Your act?"

"I didn't want to hurt your feelings, but since you stopped me, I can no longer lie." She pointed to the bed and made a circle with her finger. "What happened there? Yeah, it really wasn't that much fun."

King jumped out of the bed and sprang for the door.

Cali squealed and bolted past the couch toward the kitchen. King jumped the couch, caught her shoulders as he landed, and spun Cali into him. Her warmth wrapped around him as she kissed him through a smile. He lifted her up, fell backward over the back of the couch, and landed with a laugh. He held her tight as she lay on top of him.

"So what's protocol now, Mr. Special Agent?"

"Forget about you as soon as you walk out that door."

She kissed him.

"Yeah, is that right? And are you a 'by the books' kind of guy?"

She kissed him again.

"I've never met a rule I didn't try to break."

She kissed him deeper, but before it could go any further, reality came swiftly. His cell phone began ringing on the kitchen table.

"Wow, right on cue," she said. "Remind me never to tempt fate again."

He kissed her again, then slid out from under her. It was the last thing he wanted to do, but he couldn't let a few moments of fun interfere with the biowar someone was trying to wage against his country. A private number, always the case, was flashing on the phone's screen.

"Hello?"

"X, it's Director Lucas. We're going all in tonight." The tone in the director's voice made him sound unsure. It didn't breed confidence.

"You're going to have to be more specific."

Cali went in the other room to give him his privacy.

"Can the sheriff figure out where Kuznetsov is staying under his Doctor Semenov alias?"

"He probably already knows. You sure you want me to

speed things up that much? Once Kuznetsov misses a check-in, they're going to know something's up. This will be my last night here."

"We are aware. You've got to find everything that is being hidden in Barrow tonight."

Zero to sixty. That's the way it works most of the time in the spy game, as King had come to learn. For a year he was mostly dormant in London, then the shit hit the fan in one day. Seemed as though that was going to be the case here as well. But at least he didn't have to spend a year in Alaska. On the other hand, Cali would have been a nice fire amongst all the snow.

"I'll call the sheriff and see if I can get to the virologist before he goes to Volkov tonight."

"I'll work on getting you a plane."

"Hold on," King said. Then he hit mute on the phone. "Cali?"

Cali walked back into the main room. She was pulling her shirt down over her head. "Do I need a plane from the CIA tonight?"

"It's going down tonight?"

King nodded.

"No, you have a ride."

King unmuted the call. "Already got that taken care of. Anything else I should know?"

"We just got word that a ton of people in a town called Atqasuk, about a hundred miles from you, have been mysteriously getting sick. So far it seems consistent with the other two town disasters. We have to stop this now or the next city will be in the continental United States. Even though it is awful to lose these people in these towns, at least it's isolated. If this makes it into a spreadable area, the numbers will be catastrophic."

The news Director Lucas was laying on King was heavy. He'd been part of plenty of lifesaving missions in his day, but nothing like this. This was an intense amount of pressure. If he didn't succeed tonight, it could be the disaster his country had been fearing for decades. In the back of his mind he hoped what he found would make all of this a big misunderstanding. That somehow they were getting it wrong and Kuznetsov wasn't in on a scheme to harm the world. But with all that was going on in Barrow, coupled with the shit Sam was wading through in Moscow, it all seemed to be lining up. Someone was about to wage an invisible war from the shadows, and King needed to put a bright light on all of that darkness.

"If that was a pep talk, you're really bad at pep talks," King said.

"Probably so. Either way, gather what you can tonight and get the hell out of there. We might need you in Moscow if you're up for more in the morning."

"It's what I do."

"Good luck, son. The president and I have full faith in you and Sam."

"That was a little better. Maybe lead with that next time."

King ended the call and looked at Cali. "You mind giving Josiah a call. I'm going to need him."

"Not sure I can do anything until you put some pants on."

King's mind had already moved past the fun and games. After the call with Director Lucas, he was locked in on the task at hand. "Tell him if he has a man he can trust that's good with a gun, we could use him too."

Cali nodded and went for her phone.

King did what he always did when the shit was getting real. He scrolled to Sam's number on his phone and gave her a call.

22

MOSCOW, RUSSIA, 9:52 P.M.

SAM BIT down on the leather belt between her teeth and pounded on the round wooden table she was sitting beside. She spoke with her teeth clamped to it. "Good God, Patrick! I asked you to remove a bullet, not dig through my bloody shoulder to China!"

The small apartment smelled of rubbing alcohol and dried blood. Sam took another swig from the bottle of vodka the agent-in-place kept on hand.

It wasn't helping.

"I'm not a surgeon, Sam. Doing the best I can."

Sam had met Patrick back at Langley a time or two. He seemed to be a nice enough man. He was a big guy, large broad shoulders, a full brown beard to match his fluffy brown hair. If it wasn't for his last name, one would think he was Russian. Director Lucas had linked them up, and Sam drove straight to his apartment, after ditching the SUV for a more inconspicuous vehicle, of course, as well as picking up some essential supplies for the makeshift surgery.

"Do better," she said, just before chomping on the belt once again.

The tools Patrick was forced to use were obviously not medical grade. And at the moment, it felt like the large set of tweezers he was digging insider her shoulder were scraping bone. Patrick had been a medic for the Army in a former life. How he went from medic to CIA agent was a story Sam had yet to hear.

"Take another drink of vodka," he said in a horrible Russian accent.

"You think this is the time for humor, do you?" A bolt of pain zapped her shoulder as she watched him clamp the tweezers. "Ah! For fuck's sake!" Sam spit out the belt. The bullet sliding out felt like a tooth with an unnaturally long root being extracted. But finally, as Patrick held up the bullet with a big, dumb, happy look on his face, the pain began to subside.

"Proud of yourself, are you?" she said.

"Is that a thank-you?"

Sam pulled the second shot glass that sat a few feet away on the table over beside her own. As blood ran from the hole in her shoulder, she picked up the bottle of vodka and poured two shots. "No, this is. Cheers to you not killing me."

Patrick raised his glass, they clinked, then they both slugged back their shots. "God, this shit's nasty."

"You sound like—" Sam stopped herself before the name Xander left her mouth. The two of them were still so close, at times she forgot people were still supposed to be think he was dead.

"Who's that?" Patrick said.

"Never mind. Thank you."

"Don't thank me yet, I still have to get you stitched up."

Just as Sam was rolling her eyes, her phone began to ring. "Just sew it up while I'm on the phone. I need some sleep, so let's get this done."

Patrick unwrapped the tampon from the box Sam had picked up. He told her a tampon was about the best thing for the wound because it would expand and stop everything up.

Sam picked up her phone and answered. "Go ahead."

Alexander King's voice came through. "How you holding up, old girl?"

"I've been worse."

"They getting you fixed up?"

Sam looked at Patrick. "You could say that. I'm assuming you aren't calling just to see if the bullet was finally the end of me."

"No, you're too stubborn to die from a measly gunshot wound. I just spoke with Lucas, I'm making a run at it tonight. Here in the next hour actually."

"He told me there was a new outbreak not far from you. You'd better get out of there before they infect Barrow just to leave no trace of evidence."

"I still can't believe this is happening."

"Believe it, X. I'm fairly certain the vials Zhanna and I intercepted were headed for mass production. I have zero proof of that, it just seems the next logical step. Any info on mysterious things flying in and out of the airport there?"

"Maybe."

She didn't know why King didn't elaborate, she just knew he couldn't in that moment. Someone was listening who might be involved somehow. Years of spending weeks at a time with someone lends these types of intuitive powers.

"Okay, no need for me to know as long as you do. But I do need to know what to do next after I get Zhanna and hopefully the two vials she had back."

"I'll have a lot more information by the time morning comes for you."

Patrick slid the needle through her skin without warning. Sam grunted and gritted her teeth.

"Yeah, sounds like you're just fine, Sam," King said with a laugh. "I'll let you get to it. Talk soon."

Sam ended the call as Patrick laced her up. "Doing good, Sam. Almost finished."

"Try not to make my shoulder look like one of your American footballs, would you?"

Patrick pulled the last thread, tied it off, and cut the stitch. "It won't take much to reopen this, so try not to get into any fights." His grin told her he knew that wasn't possible.

"That's like telling a drunken Brit to lay off the gin."

Patrick poured for them this time. They clinked shot glasses again. "I'd tell you cheers in Russian, but who the hell knows what that is? And we'll have to open this and restitch in the morning to take the tampon out."

"Glorious," Sam said.

Sam set down the glass, stood, and gave Patrick a pat on the shoulder. "Don't finish that bottle. We've got business early."

"Yes, boss."

Sam didn't know a lot about Patrick. The only rumor running through the agency was that he had one hell of a temper. The teddy bear who'd just repaired her arm didn't seem to match the chatter. As she slid into bed for a couple of quick hours, she prayed to the clandestine gods that she was wrong. She and Zhanna were going to need the grizzly bear instead.

23

Josiah and King sat in the front of the sheriff's personal truck. The snow was falling over the small town at one of the northernmost inhabited places on earth. Cali was in the backseat. She wasn't happy that they were dropping her off, but this wasn't the movies. Civilians don't tag along on clandestine missions into the depths of danger. She handed King's phone back to him.

"I put my number in there. When you're ready, I can be at the airport in ten minutes. Like I told you, I can wait there if you need me to."

King turned around in the seat. "No need for that. I have no idea how long this will take."

"All right. Guess I'll just sit inside and think about earlier."

Even though Cali made a mood-lightening comment, he could see the concern in her eyes.

"Jesus, really?" Josiah said. "I try for years and James Bond rolls into town and that's it? Just like that?"

Cali flashed Josiah a killer smile. "No hard feelings, Josie."

Then she took King's face in her hands and gave him a long kiss. The last thing he wanted to do was leave her, but he had no choice.

Cali finally let him go, forced a smile, then pulled her hood up over her head as she pushed the truck door open. The cold air blasted inside the warm interior. She was off to her front door without another word.

"You lucky dog," Josiah said as he put the truck in drive.

King's mind had already moved forward. "You said the lady you knew who rents the houses said Dr. Semenov's, aka Dmitry Kuznetsov's, place was just a mile down this road, right?"

"Yep, be there in two minutes."

"Good. When you drop me off, head back to the station and wait for my call."

"No chance. You said he probably has people watching over him, right?"

"More than likely," King said.

"Then I'm not leaving you there alone."

"Trust me, this is the easy part."

"Doesn't matter, X. I told the president I was helping. That's what I'll do."

"No, you told the president you'd offer your services to me. After you drop me off, I no longer need your services. I don't know your training. I can't risk you messing up and red flags getting thrown up. I mean no offense, Josiah. But it's safer for you and me if I go it alone. If Kuznetsov isn't there, I'll only be a minute."

"Then at least let me sit a block away. Let you know if I see anything funny. And that way I'll be there when you're finished without you having to wait around for any more trouble."

As much as King didn't like it, Josiah's proposal actually did make the most sense. Whether he could actually shoot, fight, or whatever else didn't really matter if he was just the getaway driver.

"Here we are," Josiah said as he let off the gas.

"No," King said roughly. "Keep driving."

"You see something?" Josiah went back to the gas.

"No, but you can't drop me off right in front of the house. We're not serving a warrant or questioning a witness here, bud. We don't exist, remember?"

"Shit. I'm sorry."

"Now you understand why I'm going alone. But you can wait right where you drop me off. The less movement we have the better."

"This apartment complex right here should be good."

"Yeah, that'll work. Just pull under the covered parking. This may not be your police vehicle, but people around here still know your truck."

"Right. Good call."

Josiah pulled under a sheltered parking area. There were several other cars, all four-wheel drive, there as well, which was good for cover.

"If I call, it means I'm in trouble. Otherwise, I'll come straight back here when I'm finished."

"I'll be ready. And I've got a good view of the road from here," Josiah said, then squinted as he looked out the window. "Well, if the snow doesn't get any heavier than this, that is."

It was near a whiteout as it was. King supposed that living here as long as Josiah had, maybe he had special ability to see through it. King wasn't looking forward to getting out of the truck. But as far as that went, he didn't remember the last time he wanted to walk into a dangerous situation under any circumstance. Want and need were two things he had become a lot better at differentiating. Except maybe, for instance, like with Cali. His want got the better of him there.

"Be back shortly," he told Josiah.

"Be safe."

King did as Cali had a few moments ago and pulled his hood around his head. But as soon as he stepped outside into the subzero temperature, with frozen snow beating down on what little exposed skin he had on his face, he wasn't sure the hood was any help at all. The cold moved through him like a fresh needle through the skin. Only ten times as sharp. His entire body shuddered as he ducked his head down and began the short walk diagonally across the street to the house that perhaps held clues on how to stop millions of people from dying.

The only thing going through King's mind, however, was whether or not his toes would be salvageable after this mission from the frostbite that would surely greet him at the end.

24

KING FELT AS IF HE WERE ON A MOVIE SET AS HE WALKED toward the house where the infamous virologist was staying. The snow was coming down almost comically thick, as if a snow machine had gone faulty. However, there was no director there to yell cut, no matter how much King wished there was. He used to think the winters in Kentucky could have stretches where it seemed a frozen tundra. But he wouldn't have that opinion any longer. Not after seeing, and *feeling,* what real cold was like.

A man just being out for a walk in weather like this would send up red flags if someone were watching. There was no one on the roads at that point—and certainly no one but him dumb enough to be on foot. This being the case, as much as he wanted to head straight for Kuznetsov's house, he walked right on by. He squinted through what seemed a blanket of white until he saw the street behind the house. He made a left there.

King had been contemplating how to go about entering the house. There was a good chance Kuznetsov was there.

According to his security pal Arnie, Kuznetsov mostly came in to work at night. Just like he had last night. Best-case scenario, King could get in, find Kuznetsov's key card, and get out unnoticed. That way, he could head directly to Volkov and rush through to the secure room like a bull in a china shop, and then make a break for it. However, with the snow going the way it was, there would be no way Cali could fly him out of Barrow. That might be where the sheriff could actually help him. First things first, he needed the key card. The rest would have to wait.

King walked up to the back door. Visibility was only a few feet, so even finding the back door had been difficult. And he was lucky he could see even that well. If he wasn't in the middle of the only two hours of the day with sunlight, he wouldn't be able to see his hand in front of his face. A strong wind whipped through as he shielded his eyes to look through the window. He was looking into the kitchen. Sitting out on the countertop were some deli meat, mustard, cheese, and bread. Beside those things were a plate and knife. King eyed the rest of the room. No sign of Kuznetsov but he was clearly home. King would have to move to plan B.

Just as King was about to reach for the back door on his left, his cell phone starting vibrating in his pocket. He almost let it go to voice mail. Instead, he crouched and pulled out the phone. It was a local number.

"What is it?" King answered in a whisper.

"A truck just drove by," Josiah said. "I couldn't see through the snow, so I pulled out behind it. They pulled into your driveway there. I'm parking now. I'll come up the front!"

"Just park and stay in the car. DO NOT come near this house. You understand?"

"But I saw three guys getting out. You can't—"

"Stay in your truck!" he shouted in a whisper.

King put away the phone. Though he didn't need the small-town sheriff, the information he'd just relayed was extremely helpful. Instead of trying the back door, he walked around the side of the house toward the front. King had a knife in his right front pocket and his Glock tucked in a concealed hip holster—the same two friends he carried to every party of this sort.

He rounded the front of the house. The three men were just being let inside.

"Excuse me!" King shouted. "Little help here!"

All three men jerked around at the same time. They didn't pull any weapons, but King could tell by the way their hands instinctively moved toward their hips that they were packing. These men were clearly Kuznetsov's protection detail. One of them shouted something back in Russian.

"My car broke down 'bout a half mile back. Can I get a ride? Or at least use your phone? It's freezing out here!"

King continued walking toward them. One of them shouted even more loudly and certainly with more aggression. Then he took a step toward King.

"I'm sorry, man, I can't understand you. I just need a phone if you could?"

An old man finished putting on a coat and stepped outside. He said something to the men, then spoke English with a heavy Russian accent. "You cannot be here. Please go."

"Oh, thank God, you speak English!" King took a couple

of steps closer. He was in striking range of the first man of the three from the truck.

The man made a move toward King, but the old man put his hand on the man's chest to stop him. "Here! Just make quick call, then get moving. Understand?"

The old man, who King could now see was clearly Dmitry Kuznetsov, stretched his arm forward, a phone in his hand.

"Oh, thank you so much!" King stepped forward. He reached out for the phone, but instead of taking it, he chopped sideways and hit the first security man in the throat. Before the second guy in line could react, King threw the crown of his head forward and busted the man right in the nose. King used his head to strike so his hand could reach for his knife. As he moved forward, he thumbed open the blade and jammed his knife into the third man's stomach. There were a lot of great tactics in fighting, but few were more effective than the element of surprise.

As soon as his blade ripped through the man's coat and into his stomach, King retracted it and stabbed him in the neck. As blood began turning the snow below their feet red, Kuznetsov backpedaled into the house and slammed the door. King wasn't concerned about him getting away. There was nowhere to run in the blizzard. However, he did have to worry about him coming back with a gun.

But that would have to wait.

The first man had recovered enough from his neck trauma to pull his pistol. King had anticipated this and already turned toward him. As the man brought the gun from his waist, King stepped inside his arm reach and grabbed him by the coat collar. The man squeezed off two shots that burrowed into the house behind them. King lifted him off his feet, turned him over, and dropped him straight on his head. As soon as King let go of the man's coat, he turned and took a strong fist to the forehead. The man with the busted nose had momentum and rushed King, knocking him off his feet. The two of them slid to a stop in the snow, the last of the security men riding on top of him.

As King trapped the man's arm, bucked his hips, and pushed to roll over on top of him, he heard Josiah in the distance shout, "*Freeze.*" The man who was now on the bottom threw a punch with his left hand at King's head. King moved his head to the right, dodging it while simultaneously trapping the arm by the man's neck as he wrapped his own arm around the man's neck and under his head. King began to squeeze the man's arm and neck together, which worked as a blood choke. The more pressure King put on, the quicker he went out. A second later, the man went limp.

"I said freeze!" Josiah shouted again as he ran up on them.

"And I said stay in the truck!" King said as he got to his feet.

The snow had let up a bit, and in the light from the front of the house, King watched Josiah take in the three men lying on the ground.

"Put your gun away. Kuznetsov is inside. You cannot shoot no matter what he does. We can't take the chance of losing him!"

"But I heard gunshots." Josiah was a step behind.

King didn't have time to waste on explaining what had just happened. He searched the ground until he found his knife. He picked it up and walked back over to the man he'd just choked out and knelt over him.

"What are you doing? He's already out!"

King jabbed the knife twice into the man's neck where King could be sure he wouldn't wake up.

"You can't—"

"Dead men don't come back to kill you, Josiah!" King shouted as he moved over to the man he'd dropped on his head a minute ago. "This is the last time I'll say this!" King knelt down and dealt the man the same fate as his other two comrades. "This is not police work." King stood and walked over to Josiah. "If you don't understand that, you need to leave right now. I can use their vehicle now, so just go!"

Gunshots rang out from the doorway to the house. Josiah had distracted King just long enough to keep him from making it back to Kuznetsov. As King dove headfirst into the snow, he just hoped it wouldn't cost Josiah his life.

25

SEVERAL MORE SHOTS RANG OUT. KING ROSE UP FROM HIS prone position on the frozen ground. He squinted through the snow, and all he could see was a figure crouched low, arms stretched out in front. Panic bolted all through King. He jumped to his feet, took two long strides, and dove at Josiah, landing on top of him. Josiah's gun had gone off once. King sent up a silent prayer that it was not on target.

As King raised up on top of Josiah, Josiah was already beginning to protest. King could not afford this distraction. He dropped an elbow onto Josiah's forehead, and Josiah went limp beneath him. King turned toward the front door. It was open and there was blood in the snow just in front of it. King's stomach dropped.

He pulled his Glock from its holster and moved forward. "Kuznetsov! Put your gun away. Don't make me shoot you!"

King stood at the foot of the doorway. He could feel the warmth of the inside meeting him there. The house was quiet. As far as King could tell, there was no blood on the tile floor just inside. That was a good sign. It must have just been blood from one of the other men. Hopefully Kuznetsov wasn't hit. King moved in a couple more feet and shut the door behind him. He didn't hear a thing. The smell of ham wafted from the kitchen. King checked the tile and could see moisture from the melted wet snow Kuznetsov had picked up from outside.

Step by step, King followed the water trail. It went past the couch on the left, and curved through an open door on the right. King wasn't able to see the gun Kuznetsov was firing, but it had the sound of an old revolver. He hoped that was the case because he'd fired four shots outside. That would leave him with only two rounds. King was confident he hadn't had time to reload.

There was a five-foot-tall fake tree in a pot just outside the door where the water was leading him. King eased over to it, picked it up, and tossed it through the door, shouting, "He's in here!"

Two shots fired from what looked like a bedroom, followed by a series of clicks. It had in fact been a revolver, and now King could move toward Kuznetsov without fear of being shot. He did just that, pushing the door the rest of the way in and aiming his gun forward. He found Kuznetsov in the corner and was just able to jump to his right as a lamp flying his way crashed against the wall instead.

The revolver came flying next.

"You can stop throwing things now. I'm not going to shoot you."

"Tell that to your man outside." Kuznetsov's accent was thick.

The bedroom was lit with a yellow lamp from the left corner. The one he hadn't thrown. Kuznetsov had Albert

Einstein crazy white hair and a nose that could be seen from the moon. It looked even bigger in person.

"He won't be trying again. Trust me," King said.

"What do you want? They told me you would come for me."

"Who's *they*?" King had yet to lower his gun. Just in case.

"I'm just an old man, trying to help out your country. I never wanted any of this."

This wasn't the direction King had anticipated the conversation going. He'd been in this situation many times. Rarely was the man with the gun being held on him telling the truth. King had to sift through the bullshit, and he needed to make it quick.

King made a production out of putting away his gun, hoping to make Kuznetsov let down his guard. "Look, I don't have a lot of time. So I need you to be straight with me. As long as you do that, I promise I won't hurt you."

"Promises," Kuznetsov said with a laugh. "People in your line of work rarely keep promises."

"True. But despite that fact, I do promise you if you don't tell me everything that's going on here and who's behind it, I'll kill you."

Kuznetsov looked King in the eyes for a moment. "That, I believe."

"Let's get to it then. I'll split that ham sandwich with you over the details."

Kuznetsov walked around the corner of the bed, past King, and out into the living room. "Forgive me, but I have lost appetite."

"Good, then let's get down to business."

The front door creaked open, and King pulled his gun. "Josiah? Put your gun down."

The door opened further, and Josiah stepped in, holstering his gun.

"You have to get back to the truck."

"Why'd you hit me? I was trying to protect—"

"Josiah. Get the hell out of this house or I'll shoot you. I don't have time for games."

Josiah nodded and walked back out.

King put the gun away and faced Kuznetsov. "All right. Let's start with the *who*."

"You really don't know, do you?"

King didn't like that question. "If I knew, I wouldn't be standing here."

"Well then, we are both confused. Who do you work for?" Kuznetsov said.

"The United States."

"Yes, of course. More specifically the CIA, no?"

King didn't answer.

"Yes, well, we work for the same people. This is no surprise. Like I said, men in your line of work are rarely honest. Seems someone has not been honest with you."

"You're making some pretty big accusations. You mind showing some proof?"

King wasn't all that surprised yet. People tend to come up with crazy things in order to conceal what is actually happening.

"Accusations?" Kuznetsov said. And to King, he seemed genuinely surprised. "What is it you think I am doing here?"

"I'm not the one answering the questions. Get to it or I'll just take your key card and go down to Volkov Mining and find out what's behind door number three for myself. Start from the beginning."

Kuznetsov sat down on the couch. King walked around it to face him.

"I came to Seattle for conference," Kuznetsov paused and looked up at King. King nodded. "I had lunch with Nigel Warshaw, the software—"

"Yeah, I know who he is. Go on."

"When we finished lunch, he handed me a note. All Warshaw said before he left was that he hoped I would help, because his country needs it. I had no idea what he meant. The note said to wait five minutes and someone important would come to my table. When a man walked up with two men in black suits beside him, and introduced himself as Robert Lucas, the director of the Central Intelligence Agency, I realized then why Warshaw said what he did."

The hairs on the back of King's neck stood on end. He did his best not to let his mind race and jump to conclusions.

"And what did the director of the CIA want with a Russian virologist?"

"I am much more than just virologist. And shouldn't you know what your boss wanted from me?"

"Robert Lucas is not my boss. Stop assuming and keep explaining."

Technically, Lucas *was* his boss, but King was sent to Alaska by the president himself.

"I just did explain. I took more money from Lucas than I could make in a lifetime, and they took me here. I told him if he had the virus, I could discover a vaccine."

King was quiet for a moment. He walked over to the window and watched the snow. It had trailed off a bit but was still coming down. He unzipped his coat. He was beginning to sweat. What Kuznetsov was saying wasn't adding up at all. King turned back to him.

"So you're telling me that the US government paid you to come here, in the middle of nowhere, under an alias, all so they could have you doing something good, like making a vaccine?"

"Yes. Exactly. But for a virus that doesn't yet exist."

26

King stared blankly at Kuznetsov for a moment. His mind was pinging all over the place. He needed to consolidate all the information Kuznetsov was giving him and somehow make sense of it all. He was telling King that Director Lucas paid him to create a vaccine for a virus that had yet to hit the public. So what did that mean if it were true? That the US also created a virus? Or someone did and they managed to intervene and get a hold of it, but now they were scrambling to make a vaccine just in case it ever got out? If that was true, then who was supposed to be testing out the vaccine on the two small towns where everyone died?

King watched Kuznetsov cross his legs casually. He certainly didn't look like a man who was worried about his situation. Did he really believe he wasn't doing anything wrong? King had to start drilling down on this.

"Why are there so many Russians here now? If you were brought here by the US simply to create a vaccine for a virus that no one knows about, why would there be a need for so many Russians? Like the three men lying dead outside?"

Kuznetsov cleared his throat. "From what I was told, they hired a private group for security. They got them from Russia to help keep things quiet in United States. They even gave me three scientists to help with vaccine."

"They all Russian too?"

"Two Russian, one Chinese."

"You do get how this looks from my perspective, right?" King said.

"I do. But I cannot help perspective, only reality."

"Okay, tell me what you've been sending out?"

"Sending out?"

"Yeah, samples of the vaccine, the virus? I want to know it all."

For the first time, Kuznetsov squirmed. Somehow that question had made him uncomfortable.

"This has been a problem for me. I have spoken up several times, but nothing has been done. I almost cleared everything out and left last night, but I couldn't do it. I have no idea what they would do to me if I just left."

King's mind flashed back to last night when he first saw Kuznetsov standing outside. More importantly, he distinctly remembered the worried look plastered on his face. What Kuznetsov was saying and what King read in his expression last night were adding up. Could he really be telling the truth?

"What has been the problem, Kuznetsov?"

"Oh, yes. The other scientists have been pushing me for the vaccine. They have been taking samples of it before it was ready. They said they just had to send progress reports, but I knew I could do that without samples. Sample would do no one but me any good. I am only one who could look at it and know what was right and what was wrong about it."

Kuznetsov paused for a minute while he scratched his head.

"If you're thinking about not telling me something, that's a bad idea. I'm the good guy. But I think you and I both know whoever has you doing this, and those other scientists, probably aren't more good guys."

"You think that is true? That I have been doing something for someone sinister?"

"Don't know," King said as he took a seat on the couch beside the virologist. "That's why I'm asking so many questions. I have until morning to figure this out."

"What do you mean?"

King felt like he could push here and go all in. Mostly because Kuznetsov wasn't going to leave his side, so there was no one he could update if he was on the wrong side of this. The side that might be trying to kill a whole lot of Americans.

"We believe that whatever you're working on is going to be used as a weapon. To kill thousands, if not millions of Americans."

King watched as Kuznetsov jerked back in surprise. His mouth hung open as he shook his head. If he was acting, he was damn good at it.

King went on. "So, I need you to tell me what you just hesitated to say. I have to know everything so my team can stop it."

This time it was Kuznetsov who was assessing King. He gave him a long look, as if he too was trying to decipher the truth, and what side King was really on.

"They didn't know that I knew, but they also took samples of the virus."

"Who?" King said.

"The scientist and one other man who has left with those samples more than once."

King's mind jumped to the two towns that were devastated by the unknown virus. Someone had taken the virus there and unleashed it. And it had to be connected to what Kuznetsov was telling him. There was almost a surefire way to know if all of it actually was intertwined.

"I need a timeline. If you can tell me each time the virus was sampled and taken out of your lab, and they line up with other information I have, I'll walk you out of here tonight and find a way to keep you safe. Do you know how many times this has happened, and when?"

A smirk formed on Kuznetsov's face. "Nothing happens in my lab without me knowing. And I am a scientist, I document everything."

Kuznetsov rose from the couch. King stood with him. "If I show you this, I have your word you won't kill me?"

"Seeing as though men in my line of work rarely keep their word, I'm not sure what good it would do."

"Right. Well . . . you did save me from that man shooting me outside."

"Yeah, but I did that just so I could make you talk before *I* killed you."

Kuznetsov laughed. "Honesty. All right. Maybe I can trust you."

"Whether you can or not, you know that doesn't really matter. I'm all you've got."

Kuznetsov nodded. "This, unfortunately, is true. My

notebook is in bedroom. I can show you when they took the samples."

King nodded toward the bedroom for him to go. "Don't try climbing out any windows. I'm faster than I look."

As soon as Kuznetsov left the room, King pulled out his phone and dialed Cali.

"You all right?" she answered.

"When was the last time your dad flew to Atqasuk?"

"Atqasuk? Why would you want—"

"Please, I don't have time to explain."

"I-I don't know. But I can ask him."

"And I need to know who he flew there. At the very least a description of what he or she looks like."

"O-Okay. I can do that. Give me a couple of minutes and I'll call you back."

Kuznetsov walked back into the room.

"Cali, how well do you know your father?"

The question gave King a chill. The horrible situation with his own father came flooding back to him. He shook it from his mind and tried not to let his own experience muddy what he was trying to accomplish.

"I mean, we live together, X. I know everything he does, and vice versa."

"And you've never seen anything that would make you think he's doing something wrong . . . or illegal?"

"Where is this coming from, X—"

"Just answer the question!" King shouted and immediately regretted it. But he needed an honest answer.

Cali was quiet for a second. "Okay, okay. I know you're in a tough spot. I'm telling you, my dad is a good man. He just flies people where they tell him to take them. He doesn't ask questions. But he does log all his flights. I'll ask him about Atqasuk and call you right back."

"Thank you."

King ended the call. Kuznetsov took a seat on the couch and opened his notebook. "Everything all right?"

"Peachy," King said. "Now tell me what you have about the samples of the virus leaving your lab."

27

KUZNETSOV THUMBED THROUGH THE PAGES OF THE NOTEBOOK, dog-earring a few of them. King noticed his own leg was bopping up and down in anticipation of what Kuznetsov was going to say. If it all lined up, he had a lot of information to work with on what exactly was going on there in Barrow.

"All right. First time virus sample was taken was January 7."

Alarm bells rang. King's meeting with the president at the speakeasy about coming to Alaska was the day after his inauguration on January 22. By that time, the first of the small towns had been ravaged. The timing lined up. Check.

"Let me see . . . yes, the second time virus sample was taken was two weeks later."

Bing bing bing. More alarms. While King was just getting to Barrow, Director Lucas had informed him that a second town had been getting sick. Two for two. There was little doubt left in King's mind that Kuznetsov was telling the truth, and that the viral outbreaks were stemming from his work. One more big one to go.

"And then just a week later, more samples were taken."

Bingo.

"Then the last ones just two days ago."

The samples Sam ran into in Moscow. Kuznetsov had hit on all the instances King knew about. Every single one.

Kuznetsov went on. "And this is why I almost left last night. I was beginning to be very concerned about why this was happening, and if I was being told the truth." He looked up from his notebook and pointed to King. "Now I know for sure. And I should have left last night."

"I'm glad you didn't. Because now we have a chance to stop this thing. Let me ask you this. Each time the virus samples were taken, did they also take vaccine samples?"

"Yes."

"And each time they took the samples, was it after you'd made some significant discovery or progress?"

Kuznetsov stared off into space for a moment. "Well . . . yes. I believe this is true."

That's all King needed to know. It was clear to him that they were taking the samples, both of the virus and the vaccine, and going to the remote towns to test it. He needed one last hole to be filled.

"Each time the samples were taken, was there someone on the team who consistently left for a period of time?"

"Yes, every time. I have made note of this as well. One of the scientists, Doctor Abramov. He left every time, and is still gone from a few days ago."

"He's letting the virus loose and then testing the vaccine."

"Testing it? On . . . people?" Kuznetsov was appalled.

"Yes, and so far it hasn't worked.

"That is because it wasn't ready before."

"Before?" King leaned in. "Meaning you think it is now?"

"I *know* it is ready now. It has not been tested on humans, but our animal tests are 100 percent. It stops the virus from being contracted every time."

A revelation hit King like a ton of bricks. This virus and vaccine wasn't about a weapon. At least not at its inception. It was about money. Someone created a virus so they could sell a vaccine.

King's phone began ringing, breaking his train of thought. It was Cali's number. "What'd your dad say?"

"He said he flew a guy to Atqasuk just a few days ago, someone he'd taken to a couple of other places before. Does that help?"

"More than you know. Thank you. I'll call you back."

King knew all that he needed to know about what was going on in Barrow. And now he knew that whatever Sam got caught in the middle of in Moscow, someone there was trying to finalize a deal. That is why there were so many people there to interrupt the transaction.

"Is there any of the vaccine and virus left in your lab here?" King said.

"Yes. The only reason I stayed was to move to human testing. It's the last phase before the vaccination is complete."

"The vaccination is already complete," King said. "And someone has already been trying to move it, or sell it. But it had a little problem in shipping. Who has access to your lab?"

"Just me and the two other scientists left here in Barrow."

"They were supposed to be working today?"

"Yes, they are working right now. Getting test patients ready for trial."

King rose quickly from the couch. "They've already been doing human trials. They are going to clean out your lab. I've got to get over there now!"

"I'll get my coat," Kuznetsov said as he stood.

"You can't come with me. All the Russians they've brought here will be waiting to make sure no one else gets their hands on those samples. I'll have someone come pick you up and take you somewhere safe."

Kuznetsov rushed around the couch. "I must go with you. You have no idea what you are looking for."

King didn't like it, but Kuznetsov was right. If they were lucky enough to get to the lab before the other scientists cleaned it out, King would have no clue what to take and what to leave behind.

"Okay," King said. "But don't even think about bringing your gun. I believe you, but that doesn't mean I trust you around me with a firearm. Leave that to me."

Kuznetsov stopped for a moment and stared blankly at King. Then he nodded and went into his bedroom. King's mind shifted to Moscow. He thought about Sam saying they were holding Zhanna hostage. The reason they must have been doing that was because they needed the vials that Zhanna had in order to make their deal. Whatever their deal was. If it really was this unknown deadly virus and its vaccine, they would go to any length to get it all back. Which meant Zhanna might still be alive for a "trade."

But if she was, she wouldn't be alive for long. And Sam

would be walking right into the fire. There was no way these people would let either one of them live. The powers that be, whoever they were, wouldn't hesitate to tie off every loose end.

King couldn't let that happen.

28

THE TWILIGHT GREW BRIGHTER AS MORNING MOVED TOWARD afternoon. The snow had trailed off quite a bit, but it was still below zero. Kuznetsov's vehicle had finally started to warm after five long minutes into their drive. King was going over the conversation with Kuznetsov in his head. The biggest thing he was trying to reconcile was whether or not Kuznetsov had actually met with CIA Director Lucas. Since King believed the virus and the subsequent vaccine had nothing to do with the United States government, he figured that the man Kuznetsov met with was an impostor.

Maybe.

It wasn't that King was convinced Director Lucas was incapable of turning on his country. If he was being honest, he didn't know Robert Lucas that well at all. It didn't seem like his character to turn on his government, but King had been burned by people enough to know that almost anything was possible. The more King thought it over, though, the more the entire thing seemed orchestrated by someone either trying to cash in or trying to rise to power.

Neither seemed likely for Lucas. He was a career military man. His father had also been a wealthy businessman who left Lucas quite a bit of money. So money would not have been a motivator for the man. Not to mention, if he really were involved, after the president had sent King to Barrow, Lucas surely would have tried to have King killed. Instead, he'd been nothing but helpful, including having the president call to keep him out of jail. If he wanted everything to be all wrapped up in Barrow at Kuznetsov's lab without incident, jail would have been the perfect place to keep a skilled man like King. King wasn't at all buying into the CIA being involved in wooing Kuznetsov. However, it did raise the question, who was?

The obvious choice was Nigel Warshaw. After all, he brokered the meeting between Kuznetsov and Director Lucas. But could a man as intelligent as Warshaw—smart enough to bring a software company from nothing to billions—be dumb enough to think no one would find out that he was involved in getting Kuznetsov to help him? Had Warshaw been tricked as well? That was something King couldn't begin to investigate for the time being, so he would have to let it go. But someone needed to, and they needed to get started on it immediately. His go-to in this situation would have been Sam. But she already had her hands full. He couldn't go to Director Lucas, because his loyalty was, at the very least, in question. The only other person he could call was his tech wizard, Dbie Johnson. She didn't have any connections with government or agency people, but she knew everything there was to know about digging up information. If King could steer her in the right direction, maybe she could find something. King dialed her number.

"Hello?"

"Dbie, it's X."

"Everything okay?"

"Is it ever when I call you?"

"Right, no. How can I help?"

"I need to know everything there is to know about Nigel Warshaw. And I don't mean his life story, his net worth, or how much his wife got in the divorce. I mean the stuff he doesn't want anyone to know about."

"Okay," Dbie said. King could hear keys clicking in the background. "Can you give me some direction to start with? Anything?"

"I need to know if he has any involvement in anything that has to do with the medical field. Ownership, extravagant donations, et cetera."

"Not a problem. If he does, how deep in the dark web do I need to go?"

"All the way down the rabbit hole."

"You got it. Last used secure email for you work?"

"No, go to the next on the list. Number five, right?"

"Right. I'll send what I find your way and vanish the old email account."

"Thanks, Dbie, and sooner the better."

"Yeah, I kinda figured that."

King ended the call. If there was something going on with Warshaw, and it was out there, Dbie would find it. For now, King had to put all of that aside and focus on the task at hand. He made one more quick phone call to Josiah.

"X?" Josiah answered.

"You know anyone who's good with a rifle?"

"X, it's Barrow, Alaska. Some people here, the only thing they eat is what they've killed."

"Is that a yes?"

"Almost everyone here survives by shooting things that move, at long distances. How many men do you need?"

"All of them. Deputize as many as you can. Make sure they understand it's for their country, and that's all they need to know. Will they be willing?"

"All I have to do is tell them they are allowed to shoot Russians. They'll drop everything. That work?"

"I don't give a shit what you tell them. As long as they can shoot."

"Done."

"Get them there ASAP and wait for my call. Make sure they have plenty of ammo."

"You got it."

King ended the call.

"Sounds like you are preparing for war? You think that is necessary?"

"I have no idea what we are about to walk into. People were killed in Moscow earlier trying to get to your samples. I'd venture a guess they might be a little on edge here because of it."

Kuznetsov was quiet. As they drove toward Volkov Mining, King studied the old man's profile. He wondered why an accomplished man such as Kuznetsov would get involved in such a top secret operation in the middle of Frozen, USA. It was the only part that made some of the things he was saying hard to believe. King knew all too well that motivation was a funny thing. Some are driven by money, some by revenge, and some by simply fulfilling a sense of purpose, doing something they were convinced was good for humanity. King had met a lot of people in his time, from all walks of life, and very few of them did things out of the kindness of their hearts. This is what worried him. Kuznetsov did say he was paid handsomely, but to turn a blind eye to what seemed obvious corruption? It just wasn't adding up for King.

"Why did you come here, Kuznetsov?"

Kuznetsov glanced over with a raised eyebrow. "I told you. I couldn't pass up the money. This will be the last bit of work I ever have to do because of it."

King waited a second. "I don't buy it. Did you even check to make sure that the man you met with was actually CIA Director Robert Lucas?"

Kuznetsov shot him a look. His eyebrows were raised, and his mouth hung open a little. It certainly didn't seem like he'd ever considered it. "It's not possible. It had to have been him."

"Why?" King shifted in his seat to better face Kuznetsov. "Because Nigel Warshaw sent him? Because he had a CIA credential and a couple of 'bodyguards'? Let me guess, they don't send you checks for your work. It's strictly wire transfers, right?"

Kuznetsov may have answered, but King didn't hear him. He had just given himself a good idea of where to send Dbie next. While he knew whoever was actually pulling the strings of this entire thing would most certainly have an untraceable account sending the money, there was at least a trail. And giving Dbie a clue was like giving a hound dog a scent. Only, she could sniff around all over the world with today's technology.

"Mister X?" Kuznetsov said.

"What?" King shook his trance.

"We are almost there. Do you—"

"Pull over in this driveway. I need that bank account info

where your money has been sent. You have it on your phone?"

"No," Kuznetsov said as he pulled over. "But I can call someone who can get it for you."

"Call them," King handed over his phone. "But Kuznetsov?"

King made sure Kuznetsov looked up at him.

"Yes?"

"No Russian. Or I will kill you."

29

Washington, DC, 5:00 P.M.

President Gibbons shut the file that Director Lucas had given him on Nigel Warshaw. Before reading it, he was surprised when Lucas had told him the CIA already had a file on him. After reading it, it all made sense. And Gibbons did not like what he saw. The holdings some of his company had in labs in places like China and Japan instantly sent up red flags. He wasn't one to jump to conclusions, but this had foul play written all over it.

Gibbons picked up the phone and dialed Director Lucas.

"You've read the file?" Lucas answered.

"I see why you were watching him."

"Until Sam brought it up, the thought never even crossed my mind that he could be involved with all this."

The president stood and paced the Oval Office. "What

do you have on the Seattle holding company Sam said the plane was linked to?"

"Sithjohn Industries. Looks like they have investments in a few smaller software firms. Warshaw's name isn't listed on it. But one of his former board members has a minority stake. Not sure if that's enough to be rotten, but it's enough to make it stink."

"Sure is," the president said. "I need Warshaw on the phone immediately."

"Sir, all due respect, but I don't think that's a good idea."

"Why not? You just said yourself, it stinks."

"But we don't know anything yet."

"Robert, we don't have time for a full-fledged CIA investigation," the president said, raising his voice a notch. "I didn't send Alexander King and Sam Harrison out on this mission because I was worried about bureaucracy. Get him on the phone now."

"Sir, you are not equipped for that conversation. And frankly, neither am I. If he is involved, all we'll do is spook him. If he isn't involved, what are you going to say? What if you piss him off and he takes this public? This is the age of social media. He could bury you. And I'm not sure his political alignments are with you."

"I don't give a hairy shit if he voted for me or not. There are lives at stake here. Lots of them!"

Both men were quiet for a moment.

The president let out a sigh. "But you're right. I wouldn't know how to handle that conversation other than to accuse him. So what do we do?"

"We've begun monitoring. He moves, you'll know. And we are doing a deep dive into recent activity across all his personal and business accounts. If Warshaw has anything to do with this, we'll know. You have my word."

"All right. I just can't stand sitting here with my thumb up my ass."

"Welcome to my entire existence," Lucas said with a laugh.

The president wasn't in a laughing mood. "What about King? Have we heard from him?"

"Not yet. Last check-in, he was on his way to Kuznetsov's supposed home."

"Supposed?" the president said.

"Well, King says it's Kuznetsov. That's all I meant."

"What's his move?"

"Confirm it's Kuznetsov and get him to talk. He doesn't have a plan after that."

"All right. I want to know when you know. Got it?"

"Of course, Mr. President. I'll be in touch."

Gibbons ended the call and turned on the news. The media hadn't stopped speculating since news broke about the deaths in the small Alaskan town. The travel ban he had to place on the area didn't help matters any. It gave them even more to speculate about. This was all spinning out of control really quickly. But the thing that scared him the most was that it could get so much worse.

30

As King and Kuznetsov sat in the driveway that was just around the corner from Volkov Industries, King had finished another call with Josiah. Josiah had managed to get three other men, all crack shots according to him, to help in case King brought some trouble with him. King told him to have two of them set up at good vantage points at the airport—one with an eye on the entrance and one with an eye on the tarmac where Cali's dad's plane sat waiting. Then he wanted Josiah and his other man to come to King's current position. When they arrived, they would go on foot through the trees that led to the gates of Volkov. King's biggest concern was that what happened in Moscow would make the powers that be paranoid and they would beef up security. He needed Josiah's new deputies there in case the added guards needed taking down. He already explained this to Josiah so King and Kuznetsov could move as soon as he arrived. Josiah's truck was pulling up now.

King exited the SUV. Josiah parked and got out of the truck. The cold was immediate. It wasn't something King would ever get used to, no matter how long he stayed. The snow was just a trickle now, and it was the brightest part of the day. An hour or two from then, it would be back to a dark twilight. Josiah walked over and handed King an earpiece.

"How'd you manage these?" King asked as he put the radio in his ear.

"When a few of your buddies are out hunting around polar bears, it's good to be in constant communication. The other boys at the airport are in place. They're waiting for my call."

"You sure you want to do this? You don't have to. This could get ugly."

Josiah pulled his rifle off his shoulder and held it in his hands. "I know it's second nature for you to be working for the president, X, but it isn't for me. It means something when the commander in chief asks a favor of me."

"Yeah?" King smiled. "Matters to me too. Why do you think my frozen ass is way up here?"

"Good point. Well, we are going to start hoofing it. Give us a five-minute head start."

"Will do. Thanks, Josiah."

King reached out his gloved hand. Josiah grabbed it and shook it firmly. "My pleasure. Haven't seen this much excitement since Cali came to town," he said with a wink. "We have to get this wrapped up so you can get the hell out of here and I can get a second chance with her."

King feigned a tip of the hat. "Be careful out here. I have no idea what we are walking into."

"A hunter never really does."

Josiah and his deputy never looked back. King thought for a moment about that statement. It had been true many times in his life. No matter how much planning went into a mission, you never really knew what you were going to get. He thought maybe the Army should target hunters for their next recruiting campaign. Seemed they're a damn good fit.

He walked back over and slid inside the warm SUV. While they were waiting for Josiah to arrive, Kuznetsov had managed a call to his banker. The woman was going to send all records to a secure email that Dbie could comb through. Hopefully she could trace the account that had been wiring Kuznetsov his money for his work in Barrow. It could be a massive break in getting to the bottom of this entire science fiction nightmare. But King knew those odds were long.

"Let's get moving," King told Kuznetsov. "We can't afford to sit around any longer. We are as covered as we are going to be."

Kuznetsov pulled out of the driveway and drove toward Volkov. It was just around the bend of trees, not even a half mile. The plan was simple. King would be brought in as Kuznetsov's extra security. Since King was already a security guard there, he would have credentials and a backstory, and would have no need to make up some elaborate cover. All Kuznetsov would have to do is sell the fact that he felt in danger so he needed to add a little more security. The only problem with the plan was the men King killed in the driveway of Kuznetsov's house. No one was going to find them as King had dragged them inside. However, if they were supposed to check in with someone, there would be more red flags that everything at Volkov was compromised. All they really needed was to get through the gate, then pass the front desk. It was the only play they had.

The SUV rounded the bend. King moved his knife from his pocket, down to the right side of his left boot, just in case there was a search at the gate. Kuznetsov was beginning to fidget in his seat. The last thing King needed was for him to spook the guards. Then a sour thought crept in. What if he really was being played by Kuznetsov? What if the plan now was to tip off the guards? He's going to have to speak Russian to them. King wouldn't have any idea what they were saying. He needed an insurance policy.

King pulled his Glock from his concealed holster and showed Kuznetsov he was keeping it under his coat in his lap. "Just so we are clear on how this is going to go."

"They will kill me, too, you know."

"Listen, I'm about to tell you to relax, take a deep breath, and act normal with the guards. But before I do, you must know that if you spook them, I will kill you, and every one of them. Make no mistake, it's what I am trained to do, and I am the very best at it. So don't get any ideas."

"I thought you knew by now that I am on your side." Kuznetsov glanced over as he spoke. The gates to Volkov came into view.

"I don't know you. I am here for one reason and one reason only—to keep my country safe. You are merely a means to an end. And if you get out of line, I mean to end you."

"Fair enough," Kuznetsov said.

King didn't know if reassuring Kuznetsov that he was a stone-cold killer had eased his worry or not, but something he'd said had calmed the old man down. It was a win either way.

"There normally this many guards?" King said.

Kuznetsov must have known the question was rhetorical, because he didn't answer.

He didn't like what he saw as they drove closer. There were two large trucks blocking the gates on both sides and at least a half dozen men walking the area. It didn't really matter, however, because short of parachuting in, this was his only chance of entering the mining facility and the secret lab. All he could do was hope their story was viable to the guards. That, or hope his aim was true if they decided not to believe them.

31

Kuznetsov rolled slowly toward the gate. The snow had picked back up a bit, but visibility was still good.

"Deep breath," King told him. "It's just you coming to work as you would on any other day."

However, with the influx of security, it clearly was not any other day.

King added, "You're here to work. I am just extra security. Nothing more."

Kuznetsov didn't respond to King's coaching; he just pulled the SUV to a stop. Then King spoke to Josiah who was listening in his ear. "Josiah, if I say fire, you take down any man standing. Got it?"

"Got it."

"No hesitation now, you hear me? I will only say fire if they have to die."

"We have them in our sights. Waiting on your word."

King couldn't help but feel a little better that Josiah and his man were watching them, even though he had no idea if either of them could actually shoot. As a man holding a rifle walked over to their SUV, Kuznetsov rolled down the window. The man said something in Russian that King didn't understand. But he did understand when the man shook his head and pointed back toward the direction they came.

Kuznetsov glanced over. King thought he was going to crack. King's hand was ready to shoot for his Glock. Kuznetsov said something to the guard.

The guard shook his head and was a little more adamant with pointing behind them again.

Not good.

King stayed ready. He watched as Kuznetsov's chest was going up and down a little faster. He could tell he was getting worried. However, when he spoke again to the guard, his voice was even and he didn't sound worried. The word *fire* was on the tip of King's tongue. Ready to shout it if it came to that. So far it seemed likely that it would. Then the guard walked away to go talk with another of the men.

Kuznetsov looked straight ahead as he whispered under his breath. "No one is permitted today. I am trying to convince them to let just me go."

"No. I go, or they all die," King whispered back. "Tell them you discovered a problem with your calculations and that is why you are here early. Tell them many lives are at stake and if they don't let you through, those deaths will be on them."

"These men don't know about the virus or a vaccine!" his whisper was almost too loud. The pressure was getting to him. "They think this is a rock mining company!"

"No they don't," King said, keeping an even tone. "They don't know the details, but they know they aren't guarding this place over rocks. Tell them what I said.

They'll have to make a call to whoever put them here on such short notice. If they tell them you said something is wrong and people will die, maybe you'll get the go-ahead."

Kuznetsov took a deep breath. He wiped the sweat from his lip, and King could see his hand was trembling. The guard started back their way. Kuznetsov went to raise his arm again, but King shot his hand over and yanked it down.

"You're shaking," King whispered. "Just relax. You're fine."

Before the guard even got to the window, he was shaking his head. Kuznetsov tried to speak, but the guard interrupted him immediately and barked at him as he motioned for them to leave. Kuznetsov tried to speak again, but he was once again interrupted. King was ready for hell to break loose. One more time, Kuznetsov spoke but again was interrupted by the guard shouting at him. Then Kuznetsov surprised King.

Kuznetsov shouted, "Nyet!" and banged his fist on the steering wheel. Then he went on to shout at the guard. Before the guard could react, the man who was clearly in charge walked over, and Kuznetsov yelled at him as well. King prepared for a quick jump out of the car so he could get some cover as he shot them. Kuznetsov had done exactly what King asked him not to do, and freaked out. Now everyone was in danger.

Then King was surprised again. Instead of pointing his gun at Kuznetsov, the guard in charge pulled out a phone and stepped away. Kuznetsov sounded like a man who'd just sprinted a mile, he was breathing so hard. King wanted to try to calm him, but the other guard was still standing by the window. The cold air was swirling through the SUV now, but for the first time, King welcomed it. He was running hot as he tried to keep calm.

While the one man was on his phone and the other guard had his back turned, King quickly surveyed the rest of the surroundings. There were seven men total. If he took out the two guards who had approached the car, and Josiah and his man could get two others close to the gate, he had a fighting chance. The Suburban they were in would provide ample room for King to move behind and still be protected. The next worry would be what awaited beyond the gate. They needed whatever Kuznetsov shouted at the guards to work. It was not only the cleanest way in, but it might be the only way out. Other security would hear the shooting, and they would send more men. It would be too much for King to try to survive while keeping Kuznetsov alive as well.

Kuznetsov broke. He pounded the steering wheel again and shouted something out the window. The guard closest to him turned and pointed his gun at Kuznetsov's head. King watched the guard's eyes. He was focused on Kuznetsov, and Kuznetsov only. King slid his hand under his coat and wrapped his hand around the grip of his gun. If this was about to go down, he wasn't going to be the last man with a weapon in his hand.

The guard pointing the gun at Kuznetsov was shouting now. King readied himself by moving his finger along the trigger. He angled the gun upward, pointing it, from under his coat, at the guard's right shoulder. Kuznetsov had frozen up when the gun had been turned on him. He was holding his hands in the air and seemed to be begging for his life. The guard shouted one more time; then a man yelled at him from behind. The guard holding on Kuznetsov seemed to protest; then, after another command, he lowered his weapon. King released the breath he was holding, but he did not let go of his weapon.

The man in charge put away his phone, and as he was walking toward their SUV, he gave a waving motion and shouted something to the guards by the gate. They were going to let them in. But that meant they were going to search King. He was security, so it wouldn't be a deal breaker that he had a weapon, but if it was sitting in his lap, that would be a problem. Before the man could make it to the SUV, King slid the Glock from under his coat and quickly tucked it into the concealed holster at the small of his back. The man hadn't see him do it.

The truck in front of them roared to life, and as it moved out of their path, the gate also began to open. Step one of the secret mission had been cleared.

Next came the hard part. Extracting the evidence. King knew that however rough the entrance had just been, it was going to seem like still waters compared to getting out of there alive.

32

THE HEAD GUARD BARKED SOMETHING AT HIS OTHER MAN, who then walked around the front of the SUV. The head guard then opened Kuznetsov's door and ordered him out. King knew he would be searched as well. He waited for the guard to open his door. The guard shouted at King and pulled him out of the vehicle way too hard. King stumbled forward but managed to keep his cool. King wasn't a massive guy, but he towered over this little man, who then shoved King forward against the hood and pushed his upper body to where King's face was on the frozen fiberglass. Again, King didn't react. He would have taken a beating at that point just to get through the gates.

Then he felt a sharp pain after something slapped against the back of his head. The guard had just struck him in the head with his gun. Rage flooded King. And believe it or not, it was the sheriff who nearly shot and killed Kuznetsov an hour or so ago who actually calmed him down.

Josiah spoke through King's earpiece in a soft tone.

"Easy, X. Don't let that guy get to you. They're going to let you in if you can keep your cool."

King took a deep breath. The head guard at the other side of the truck was shouting something at the little man in Russian. It sounded like he was angry with him for hitting King on the head. That's when King felt the guard slip King's gun out of his holster. A split second later he twirled King around and was shouting at him as he pointed King's own gun at his face.

"Just say the word and we can take all these guys together," Josiah whispered.

King was ready to take more punishment for the cause, but he was not used to being on the receiving end. The man's half-covered face, spitting unmentionables in Russian, was beet red in front of him. King could see that the abuse of power he was wielding was simply a cover for his fear. His eyes told the real story.

Finally, his boss shouted something that made him cool off. The boss walked around the SUV and finished patting King down. He made the mistake of not reaching down inside King's boot, so he didn't find the knife King had tucked away there. King hoped that would come back and haunt the man before all of this was over.

The boss seemed satisfied, so they pulled King off the hood. King stared down the little man, then got back in the SUV. The two guards got in the back of the SUV, and the boss must have told Kuznetsov to drive, because that's what he did. The car now smelled of cigarettes, and all the heat equity that had built up inside was gone. But at least they'd made it past the gate.

"Nice job," Josiah whispered. "We'll be out here freezing our asses off waiting for you, so make it quick, would you?"

King appreciated the humorous jab. It helped him center himself and forget about the pip squeak behind him who'd bashed him in the head. Kuznetsov drove up to the front of the first building of what collectively was Volkov Mining. King didn't move until he was removed from the car by the guard who had assaulted him. Then the four of them moved toward the entrance. King had a feeling these two were going to be like shadows until he and Kuznetsov left the property.

The two guards swiped them in, and finally they were out of the cold. King removed his beanie, stuck it in his pocket, and unzipped his coat. As they pushed inside the second door, King was surprised and unhappy to see that Arnie was working the desk. He stood up with a look of shock on his face.

"Xavier? What the hell are you doing here?"

"Security for Dr. Semenov here. What about you?"

"Working a double. Everything okay?" Arnie looked behind King at the two security guards.

"Any idea why there is so much security here today?" King said.

"You know they don't tell us nothing."

All four of them walked past the security desk and over to the first secured door. The boss guard said something to Kuznetsov. Kuznetsov responded, then the boss shook his head no.

Kuznetsov looked at King. "He said you must stay here. I said I need you and he said—"

"No, yeah, I saw that."

When King had exited the SUV outside, he was sure to look back over his shoulder to see what was happening at the gate. He found them shutting it and pulling the large truck back in front of it. No one was coming in or out. When he got inside, as he was talking to Arnie, he checked all the monitors behind him. No other security, other than the other desk guard on shift, and he was outside building three. King knew from walking the perimeter himself that the second deskman on duty wouldn't be back for at least ten more minutes. All of that was important because it meant it was just King and the two gate guards who'd escorted them in.

He would settle for those odds every time. Especially when the guards were sure the situation was under control.

Without warning, King twisted his hips to the left and fired a right hand directly at the boss guard's nose. It shattered as he dropped backward to the ground. King turned toward the little guard who'd hit him in the back of his head outside. A look of terror formed on his face as he tried desperately to bring up his rifle, but his shoulder strap was in the wrong place and couldn't be raised any higher without taking precious seconds to move the strap.

He didn't have time for that.

King reached down and grabbed the barrel of the rifle with his left hand, simultaneously grabbing the shoulder strap around the man's neck with his right. He ripped the rifle up over his head, then push-kicked him in the stomach, sending him backward a few feet. As the guard regained his balance, he fumbled in his pocket presumably for King's own Glock. King had watched him put it there as his boss guided King into the SUV earlier. Before the man could produce the gun from his pocket, King happily returned the favor and swung the rifle like a baseball bat, making a solid connection on the side of the guard's head.

The guard subsequently collapsed to the floor. King took his gun back and slid it inside his holster.

"Xavier, what the hell are you doing, man?" Arnie shouted from behind the desk.

"Arnie, find something to tie these guys up."

"I-I can't do that. They'll fire me!"

"I don't have time for this. If you don't tie them up, I'll just shoot them. Up to you."

Arnie could see that King wasn't kidding, so he raced back to the break room. King grabbed both guards by the back collar of their shirts and dragged them into the break room and told Kuznetsov to follow him.

"What's happening? Who are you?" Arnie said as he walked back from the maintenance closet with a couple of extension cords.

"Just tie them up. I work for the US government and I need your help. Can I count on you?"

"US government? What the shit, man? You're just a security guard like me."

Arnie's chubby face was turning red.

"Arnie, did you see how I just took these guys down?"

King waited for Arnie to nod.

"Mere 'security guards' don't normally know how to do that, do they?"

Arnie shook his head.

"Arnie, your country needs you. I know you always wanted to be part of the police force. Well, now is your chance to be CIA."

Arnie perked up immediately.

"I hereby deem you a temporary agent," King went on. "Do you accept, on behalf of the president of the United States?"

Arnie nodded slowly at first, then more emphatically. "Yes, yes I do."

"Good. Now, Agent Arnold Clark." King was really playing it up. "I need you to tie these men up, gag them, and make sure Roger doesn't let them out of this room when he gets back from his building check. You understand?"

"Yes. Yes, sir." He patted the radio at his hip. "I'll give you the other radio at the desk."

"Good. And just as important, you have to tell me if someone else is coming in. Got it?"

"I can do it," Arnie said. Then he knelt down, rolled the boss guard over, and began tying his wrists. "So what's going on?"

"If you can do these things I've asked, Arnie, I'll fill you in when this is over. And I'll make sure the sheriff takes a second look at you for the force."

The look on Arnie's face was like a kid on Christmas morning. "You would do that?"

"Absolutely. So long as you don't let me down."

"I got this, Xavier . . . wait a second, that ain't even your real name, is it?" he said with a grin.

King held up his hands in a surrender pose. "You got me."

Arnie smiled and shook his head. "Mary will never believe this."

King didn't have time to give him the "*Mary can never know about this*" speech. "I'll be back shortly. Make sure no one comes in without me knowing."

"You got it!"

King turned to Kuznetsov. "Okay. It's showtime. Let's make this quick."

The two of them walked back out to the secured door.

King glanced outside and saw no signs of anyone coming. He removed his coat and laid it on the desk as he grabbed the handheld radio. Kuznetsov swiped his card, and they made their way inside. It was time to see if Kuznetsov was telling the truth about what was going on in Barrow or not. Either way, it would be information that was much needed in the next step of getting to the bottom of who was trying to weaponize a virus on American soil.

33

KING AND KUZNETSOV ENTERED THE SECURE DOOR AND walked down an empty hallway.

"Josiah," King spoke to his earpiece. "You still with me?"

"We're here."

"What's it looking like at the gate?"

"Same as after you all went in. Except the two guards who went with you never came back out."

"Yeah," King said. "They won't be either."

"Nice. Listen, I went ahead and had Cali make her way to the airport. That okay?"

"Good. I shouldn't be long. We are heading into the lab now. Let me know if anything changes out there."

"Roger that."

The two of them approached a door. This was the second one, the last door visible via the security camera system. Beyond it was where King's knowledge of the facilities ended. Kuznetsov once again swiped his key card and the door unlocked. He pushed through, and the only thing on the other side was a small room with an elevator directly in front of them. That is not what King was hoping to see. He was not thrilled about going below ground, with his only way out being an elevator, which would make it that much harder to escape if something were to go wrong.

"How far down we going?" King asked as they walked toward the elevator. This was a fingerprint-only elevator, so Kuznetsov pressed his thumb against the small screen. It turned green and the elevator door slid open.

"Are you claustrophobic?" Kuznetsov said.

"When people are trying to kill me or you over a super deadly virus and we might be a few floors underground with no way out? Well, yeah. I guess that does make me feel a bit claustrophobic. Otherwise, no. I was a Navy SEAL. Everything we did in training was underwater."

King didn't know why he elaborated with the SEAL comment. Perhaps a little nervous about being trapped down there with a deadly disease.

"Just three stories down," Kuznetsov said. "But don't worry, it's a big lab."

The elevator jolted to life and began moving down. King couldn't escape the flashing thought that he was being lowered into his grave. Fortunately, it wasn't the first time he'd had these sorts of feelings and managed to overcome the situation. It was one of the many things his training and experience had taught him over the years. Thoughts only control what happens in reality if you let them. He hadn't let a negative thought win yet, and he wasn't about to start now.

The elevator came to a stop, and as soon as the door opened, the two so-called *scientists* who Kuznetsov said would be there looked up in surprise. So did the three armed men standing guard around them. As they turned their guns toward him and Kuznetsov, King's instinct was to reach for his gun, but he stopped himself for fear that it might trigger the guards' shooting reaction. Instead, King raised his hands at the same time Kuznetsov had.

"Dr. Semenov?" A dark-haired woman in a lab coat spoke in a Russian accent. "What are you doing here? The guards at the gate radioed that you were coming. They said something about a problem?"

It was clear the scientists, or whoever they actually were, were there to close up shop.

"What are you doing here?" Kuznetsov answered, pointing at the stainless steel cases they were loading into boxes. "I didn't order these to be moved."

She stared at him blankly for a moment. The guards didn't lower their guns. Whatever was going on, it was clear that Kuznetsov wasn't in on it. And that part at least made King feel better. The problem was, if they were through with Kuznetsov, there was no reason not to kill him. And King, too, for that matter.

An Asian man in a lab coat set down what he was packing and stepped toward them. "We've been ordered to leave. Haven't you heard?"

"Heard what?" Kuznetsov said.

While they were talking, King scanned the room. It was all open, with tables filled with research and lab equipment such as beakers, microscopes, and safety gear. On the right there was a large metal locker about two feet from the wall, with lab coats and other materials stored inside.

"There was an attack in Moscow," the Asian man said. "Two women intercepted a shipment, and management is afraid it will be linked back here."

King knew the two women were Zhanna and Sam.

"Why was I not notified immediately?" Kuznetsov was incensed.

"We just assumed you were when they called us here and told us to shut it down. They called for Protocol Red. We assumed you knew because Veronika—"

The Asian man paused. King already knew why. He knew that Veronika was the name of Kuznetsov's long-time assistant. And he knew the Asian man wasn't about to offer good news. He also knew now that these two people in lab coats knew Kuznetsov's true identity. It's the only way they would know Veronika meant something to him.

"What? Veronika what? She couldn't possible have anything to do with this."

"She's . . . she's dead."

Kuznetsov's knees buckled, and King caught him before he fell. The Asian man pulled a chair over, and King sat him down. Kuznetsov began crying. But King was focused on the guard whose radio just beeped. A man speaking Russian came through its speaker. King didn't understand the words, but he understood that the men at the gate had probably been trying to reach the two guards who had escorted King inside. When they didn't respond, the men down here were probably their next checkpoint to see if everything was all right. They were about to find that out that it wasn't. King reached for his gun before the man on the radio could finish letting the guards know there was a problem.

He did so in just the nick of time.

34

THE LAB WAS QUIET EXCEPT FOR THE MAN SPEAKING THROUGH the guard's radio and the mild sobs of grief coming from Kuznetsov. Fortunately for King, the moment he'd reached back for his gun, the two other guards had their attention drawn to whatever the man on the radio was saying. But King knew that wouldn't last long.

Before anything changed, he pulled his gun and yanked on the back of the chair Kuznetsov was sitting in. It almost toppled over, but King managed to correct it and slide the chair back toward the metal locker. The woman in the lab coat screamed when she saw King's weapon. The guard on the right moved so fast that he had a clear shot, except that Kuznetsov was in front of King, which King assumed was why he didn't shoot.

Kuznetsov tried to stand up as King pulled the chair around behind the back of the locker, but King pulled him down to the ground by the collar of his coat. By then, the guards were screaming at King in Russian. King pointed to Kuznetsov and mouthed the words "don't move." Then he walked over to the other side of the locker and took a peek around. He almost lost his nose. The guard on the right began shooting immediately. Soon the bunkered lab sounded like a war zone as all three of the guards were firing. At first, the female scientist was screaming, but that quickly stopped. Since the scientists were in between King and the guards, they must have been shot.

King put his back to the metal locker as bullets clanked against it on the other side. King needed to even out the numbers, and fast. If two of the three guards came around both sides of the locker at the same time, he wasn't going to make it. He looked up above him. The locker was about eight feet tall. There was nothing behind the locker with him, but he did notice the radio that Arnie had given him clipped to his pant pocket. As one of the guards shouted in Russian at them, King took his gun and quietly slid it up on top of the locker. He bent down to Kuznetsov's level.

"Tell them we surrender," King whispered.

Kuznetsov shot him a look. His eyes were wide. He wasn't frightened, it didn't seem, but more surprised. Then he shouted a sentence in Russian. The guards did not immediately respond. This was an intense situation from all angles. But the fact that King could not communicate with the guards, nor could he understand what Kuznetsov was saying to them, only doubled the displeasure. Kuznetsov could have been saying anything to them. There was a little bit of a back and forth; then King heard the squeak of a rubber sole moving on top of the poured concrete.

They were coming.

King took the radio in his hand and threw it as far as he could out into the lab. He simultaneously lifted his foot onto the empty chair and boosted himself up the locker. He hooked his left elbow on top of the locker, and just as the radio hit something across the room in a loud crash, he picked up his Glock, found the first guard he could see, and squeezed the trigger three times. He dropped back down out of sight when the guard went down and the other two turned their guns up toward him. He was quick to the far side of the locker, and when he jumped out from behind it, he shot the only remaining visible guard twice in the chest. The guard's gun had still been firing toward the spot were King had been on top of the locker. King spun back around behind the locker and waited.

The lone remaining gun stopped firing. Whoever these men were who'd been hired as guards didn't seem like former military, and probably not even former police officers, because they had no idea what they were doing. King heard the magazine slide from the guard's rifle. He would have no way to protect himself. King took full advantage and walked around the locker with his gun extended. He had time to watch as the guard fumbled with a fresh magazine, but he would never get it loaded. King squeezed his trigger twice, and the man clutched his chest before he fell to the ground.

"We've gotta move, Kuznetsov. Get out here and gather what you need."

Kuznetsov came around the corner and took in the damage. Bodies were spread around—it was a horrible sight. Especially for someone like Kuznetsov who'd never been a part of such violence. King's ears were ringing from all the gunfire. He knew he was lucky that these men weren't more skilled. He was always surprised how often men like these were undertrained. With so many fantastic former military in the world, there really was no excuse for it. Except maybe the fact that Barrow, Alaska, didn't exactly draw skilled volunteers.

"Let's go," King prompted Kuznetsov. "Worry about the lost later. Sorry, but we have to go." Then he spoke to his earpiece. "Josiah, can you hear me?"

King watched Kuznetsov shake out of his trance and begin looking for what they needed to take with them. He heard nothing back in his ear. "Josiah, do you read me?" He wasn't surprised. The radios Josiah gave him were good, but not this far underground. He had no way to speak to Arnie either, with his radio being a casualty of the shootout.

As Kuznetsov pulled out a few vials and was putting them in the preformed foam inside a briefcase, King began nosing around. At the far wall, he noticed a desk. Since the scientific tools and such meant nothing to him on the lab tables, he walked over and took in the desk. There was a computer, several files, a printer, and a few other office supplies on top. Nothing of use. But there was one drawer that was partially open, and inside he could see a notebook. King glanced up at Kuznetsov, who was closing up the brief-case. King reached in the drawer, grabbed the mini mole-skin notebook, and shoved it in his pocket. As he learned last year in Greece, notebooks like these can be not only gold mines but also the difference in many lives being saved. It could be just the musings of an old man, but it could hold a whole lot more.

35

"Warshaw is on the move," Director Lucas said.

President Gibbons sat up in his chair and leaned toward the phone on his desk where the director's voice was coming through the speaker. Gibbons had just come out of a Homeland Security meeting with his top officials, and the only topic on the docket that day had been the new virus. Gibbons had high hopes that King and his team could stop it, but he had to plan as if they wouldn't. He could not let things get out of hand like they had when the coronavirus came to the States from China. If this deadly new virus had been COVID-19, the country would have never recovered. That's why he had no choice but to stop travel from outside the lower forty-eight states. Since hearing how the virus had traveled to the small towns in Alaska, and possibly in vials that were intercepted in Moscow, everyone in the meeting unanimously agreed.

He had to protect his citizens, regardless of the potential political and economic backlash.

"Where's he going?" the president asked.

"He and his family have left their home. We have men following him."

"So, they are going out to a late lunch? What the hell are you saying?"

Director Lucas cleared his throat. "Sorry, we also have men watching the pilot of his Gulfstream G650, who just arrived at the airport. We don't know yet, but it seems likely that's where Warshaw is headed."

If Director Lucas was correct, Gibbons didn't like the timing of this at all. His meeting about the travel ban and next steps on securing the United States had ended only thirty minutes ago. However, that was enough time for someone to get word to Warshaw that travel outside the United States was coming to an end for the time being.

"Do you think he knows about the travel restrictions already?" Director Lucas said. "Is that possible?"

"Only if there is a leak." Gibbons knew most of the men and women personally who were in that meeting. He couldn't fathom one of them could be feeding a tech billionaire inside information. Other than Director Lucas, there were only five other people in the meeting. "As soon as you know where Warshaw is going, I want to know. And if it is the airport, he can't leave."

"You got it."

Gibbons pressed the button on the phone that ended the call. His first thought was wondering whether or not he was doing enough to keep America safe. Had he made a mistake by sending in a small team to root out what was going on? He had never been one to second-guess himself, but he also had never been personally responsible for so many lives. And with Sam's meeting to try to retrieve the vials not happening until morning Moscow time, and King not checking in after making moves in Alaska, he couldn't help but worry he had let his country down. His number one job as the head of the United States was to ensure that people could safely go after their dreams with the least amount of resistance possible.

If all of them were dead, that would make it rather hard to pursue life, liberty, and happiness.

36

THE STREETS of Moscow were mostly empty. The street-lights glowed yellow, making the sky above seem all the more dark. Though Sam had gone to bed a couple of hours earlier, she never really had any intention of sleeping. Not when Zhanna was in danger. She'd snuck out of Patrick's flat and taken a cab down to the address given by the mysterious man. She had done a search for local hot spots nearby, and there was a bar open on the corner across the street. The wind was cold as it swirled around her. When she pulled her coat tight, she could feel the stitches in her shoulder letting her know they were still there.

There were a few late-night patrons coming and going from the bar as she walked by. Several cabs were picking people up and carrying them away, but overall it was fairly dead for being in the middle of a city. She stood on the corner and looked diagonally across the street. The only thing she saw there was a deli, its lights dark, and the windows even darker. Upon a more detailed look, she could see that the windows had been boarded up as if the closing had been of the more permanent variety.

Sam crossed the street when she had an opening. She moved her eyes from the first level of the building to the light that was on two stories high. Windows wrapped all the way around the building on all three levels. There were a few other lights dotted on. Above the retail space were apartments. Not an uncommon thing in a city. She wondered if Zhanna were in there somewhere.

She walked up the block to the next crosswalk and crossed over to the deli's side of the street. Most of the windows were too dark to see inside. She continued toward the deli's entrance, giving it a once-over as she strolled by. No real sign of a way in. Sam walked around to the back of the building. A man and a woman were making out, and the smell of vodka wafted all the way over to her. There was nothing else back there but some dumpsters and a few parked cars, but the smell of vodka reminded her that she could at least warm up in the bar while she thought through her next move.

When she turned around, two men were coming out of the deli. The closed and boarded-up deli. The hairs on the back of her neck stood on end. One of the men turned and locked the door behind him, while the other couldn't take his eyes off Sam. This was the point in espionage where Sam had a clear advantage over Alexander King. Sam was a beautiful woman. Though she wasn't as young as she once was, she looked five to ten years her junior. The man staring at her was clearly intrigued. A nice-looking woman, from years of experience, can spot that look a mile away. No matter how mature or intelligent a man was, he still had instincts. And his testosterone never lied. Sam flashed him a wide smile as she walked by.

The man said something in Russian. Sam turned around without stopping, held out her arms, and said, "Sorry, I only speak English."

The man's smile grew. "I speak English too," he said, his accent so thick she could hardly understand him. "You are thirsty?"

Sam looked back over her shoulder at the bar, then back to the man, and raised her eyebrow with a flirt. He said something in Russian, and now both men were looking at her like a buttered steak.

She waited for a break in the cars, then jogged across the street. The two men followed closely behind. Two young women were exiting the bar, and Sam stepped inside before the door could close. Inside the bar was nearly as dark as the sky outside. The bar top ran the length of the room on her left, and black hanging lights glowed red above every other bar stool. Booths lined the wall on the right, and four-top bar tables made up the space in between.

The bar was still half-full. Sam had no idea what time it closed, but she didn't care either. The reason she had decided to come down to the given address in the middle of the night walked in right behind her. All she was hoping for was to maybe find something to make the meeting in the morning go more her way. She couldn't help but think the two men who had just hooked their arms around hers were that very thing.

They escorted her to an open booth. Before she sat down, she looked at the handsome man who'd spoken to her outside. "I have to go to the ladies' room. I'll be right back. Maybe get a girl a vodka martini? Extra dirty?" she said with a wink.

The smile on his young face was creepy at best. He loved the extra dirty line, as she knew he would.

"No problem. Hurry back, beautiful."

She gave him a nod and walked back toward the back of the bar. The restrooms were just up ahead. As she turned the corner, she noticed someone already taking their drink order back at the booth. She stopped short of the bathroom and took out her phone. She waited there patiently with her thumb on Patrick's contact. One eye on the phone, one eye on the men. After a couple of minutes, the drinks arrived at the table. She moved behind the wall as much as she could, with one eye peeking out. Her goal with the two men was to get them drunk enough that she could steal their key. Something she could easily do, but it would take hours. She was happy to see one of the men take something out of his pocket and drop it down into her drink. If she played this right, she could be inside the boarded-up deli within an hour.

She tapped Patrick's contact. It rang twice and then a very sleepy baritone voice answered. "Sam. Sam? Are you all right?"

"Deep breath and wake up, Agent O'Connor."

"Sam, where the hell are you? I saw you go to bed."

"I'm figuring out how to get my friend back, and I think I have a way in. But I need you down here in case I'm wrong."

She heard Patrick take a deep breath and also the rustling of sheets.

"Yeah, yes . . . Why didn't you just tell me you were leaving?"

"Didn't think I would find an opportunity like this.

There's a bar across the street from the address given to us for the meeting tomorrow. Turns out it's a boarded-up deli. Anyway, I'll be here with two men who are going to carry me back to that deli in about one hour. It will look like I am drunk, drugged, or both. Just keep a watchful eye."

"Sam, we don't know who these people are. Why take the chance tonight?"

"Because, my friend might be inside, and I'm not going to just leave her there."

"Fine. I'll be down shortly. Don't leave until I get there."

"Make it quick. I don't want to fake flirt with these boys any longer than I have to."

Sam ended the call.

Now she just had to figure out a way to drink her martini without taking a single sip. It wouldn't be easy, but on a scale of tough missions, it ranked pretty low on her difficulty list.

37

KUZNETSOV AND KING walked into the elevator. Kuznetsov was holding a briefcase full of deadly liquid and its vaccine, and King was holding the dead guard's AR-15, stocked with a fresh magazine, and his Glock in the holster at his back. King fully expected the cavalry to have come from the gate after they spoke with the guard, now dead, on his radio. He was hoping his earpiece to Josiah would come back online before they were in eyeshot of the security cameras, so at least he would know what he and Kuznetsov were walking into.

"Josiah, you hear me?"

For the first time since going underground, he heard a voice come back on the radio, but it was broken. Every third word was intelligible.

"Josiah, say again?"

A couple more words could be discerned. He heard the

words *movement* and *gate*, but it didn't tell him anything he hadn't already expected. So he did the only thing he knew to do until full communication returned.

"Fire, fire, fire fire!" he shouted as the elevator reached the top floor.

Finally, Josiah's voice came in loud and clear. "We got two of them, but two made it through the gate! They'll be inside!" Josiah sounded out of breath.

"I hear you, I hear you. Any other movement?"

"We're almost to the gate. One more truck just came through. There will be more. We've gotta get out of here!"

King heard two gunshots after Josiah stopped talking. He could tell immediately they were hunting rifles.

"I got one more going through the door. Could be as many as five or six inside with you now."

King and Kuznetsov stepped out of the elevator into the tiny holding room. The last room without cameras.

King stopped Kuznetsov from walking to the door. "Will any of these guards have access to this door?"

"Only man you tied up. No one else."

That sounded good, but King didn't search him for a key card, so he still had it on him. If his men were able to bust into the break room, they could very well have freed him and could be waiting just on the other side of the door in front of them.

"Stay here," King said. "It's the safest place for you."

He didn't wait for a reply; he readied the AR-15 and opened the door. He jumped back out of the doorway, just in case, but no gunfire came. So far, so good.

"Josiah, I'm about to go into the main lobby. If you see men in a mall-cop type uniform, don't shoot them. They aren't with the other guards."

"We are at the gate, be to you in a sec."

"Negative. Hold back."

"But, X!"

"Negative." King walked forward. "I need you and your man alive. If these guys in the truck you saw driving in late have been alerted, there will be more, probably making their way to the airport just in case. Just get one of the trucks ready to go. When I need you to pick us up, I'll say fire again."

"You're the boss. I've got two more officers heading to the airport, and three more headed here. This is turning into an all-out war. You sure you don't want us coming in from behind them?"

Josiah saying what he did about a war gave King an idea. There was a way Josiah could be useful from a distance.

"Scrap what I said. Can you create a diversion?"

"What are you looking for?"

"An explosion by the entrance would be great. If not, maybe let one of those extra trucks loose on the front door?"

"Hold on, let me . . . Yeah, keys are in the truck left here."

"Can you run it into the front door of the building without being in it?"

"I can run it into the building. I'll bail before it gets there."

"Go now. Give me a three, two, one when it's going to hit. Then I'll make my move."

King heard a door slam and an engine start.

"Be there in a few seconds," Josiah confirmed.

"I'm ready."

King could absolutely use some help in his current predicament, and he was happy to have thought of a way for

Josiah to distract the guards without putting himself at risk. As he approached the door to the lobby, he looked up into the camera. He figured the longer he took to get out the door and start shooting, the more time one of the guards would have to get lucky.

He readied his rifle and placed his hand on the door-knob. He closed his eyes, and as he waited for Josiah's countdown, he pulled up the image of the lobby in his head. Fortunately, he'd spent many hours there the last week and a half. He could see every detail. Other than behind the desk, there was no place for men to hide. He figured by that point at least a couple of them had already moved into the break room to free the other two guards. There was no time to worry about Arnie, only time to focus on killing as many men as he could in the shortest amount of time possible.

"Okay, X," Josiah said.

King gripped both the door handle and the rifle a little harder. He heard a door open in his ear, some wind rustling, then a loud grunt and a shout of pain. Josiah had just jumped from the moving truck.

"Shit! Three . . ."

King pulled down on the door handle with his left hand.

"Two . . ."

King brought the AR up to eye level and bent his knees into a crouch.

"One!"

King shoved the door open and brought his left hand up to help steady the rifle. The guards inside must have already had their guns trained on the door because gunshots blared and bullets began pelting the now open door. This didn't surprise King, as he'd figured they were watching on camera. What did surprise him was just how loud the crash was when the truck slammed into the building.

King made his move. As soon as he hit the lobby, he saw the nose of the military-style truck halfway through the door. There was glass everywhere. The engine was still running, but the truck had come to a stop. It was time for King to start. One guard was picking himself up off the floor, so King squeezed twice and he went down. Directly to his left another man tried to bring his focus back to King from the truck, but it took him too long. Two more squeezes and blood erupted from the man's neck.

The rest of the lobby was hidden from King until he got to the edge of the wall on his left. As soon as he made it there, he just started shooting. At about the third shot another man came into view, but King was already filling his body with bullets. He sidled up to the wall and took a quick glance around the corner toward the doorway of the break room. He was nearly hit by a man who was ready and waiting for him with plenty of bullets. King had taken three down, and out of the corner of his eye, he saw two more who had fallen victim to the truck. That was five, the man at the door made six, and he felt fairly confident that the last two were the guards who'd come in with him who were still tied up.

"We've got another truck on the way in, Josiah." This was a new voice. It must have been the man Josiah had brought with him.

"Josiah," King interrupted. He had to shout over the man still shooting at him in the lobby. "Get the SUV ready that I drove here in. I'll be out in a second. Both of you just start shooting at the incoming truck if you have cover. Just try to buy me a minute. I just need a minute!"

King dropped to his knees, stuck his head and gun around the corner, and shot the guard in the doorway in the knees. The guard dropped to the ground, but King had no idea there was another man standing behind the guard, and he was ready to shoot. King was dead to rights. Just as he started to raise his gun, the guard's gun fired, but it was severely off line due to Arnie hitting him in the back with a chair right beforehand. Another split second and King would have been dead.

"Any more of them back there, Arnie?" King shouted.

"Just the two we have tied up, and Roger. He believes that you're an agent now, by the way."

"Both of you get the hell out of here, now!"

King turned and moved back down the hallway. "Kuznetsov! Open up! We gotta go!" he shouted as he approached the door.

The door began to open slowly. King took hold of it, slung it open, and grabbed Kuznetsov by the coat, pulling him along.

"Josiah! You're awful quiet! How we looking out there?"

King pulled Kuznetsov out into the lobby.

He didn't get an answer back from Josiah.

38

Moscow, Russia, 1:45 a.m.

The two Russian men who had walked out of the boarded-up deli about an hour before, and escorted Sam across the street to the bar, were starting to get handsy at the booth. Sam was getting tired of acting like she was a drunken slut to encourage them. So she couldn't have been happier when her fellow agent, Patrick O'Connor, finally walked through the door. She was beginning to think it had been a mistake calling him at all. She knew she could deal with the two bozos currently keeping her company. But not knowing what she might find once they took her back across the street, she was grateful he was there.

The big guy walked into the door and scanned the bar. Sam made sure she was looking at him when his eyes found her. She managed to give him a wink to let him know all was good. Patrick walked over to the bar and took a seat at one of the bar stools that could swivel enough to keep an eye on her. She had never worked with him before, so all she could do was hope he was as good as she heard he was if things went sideways.

She was about to find out one way or another.

When Sam had come back from the bar, she managed to take a full martini off a table on the way to her booth. She picked the moment when a strange man was standing near the booth she was sharing with her two gentleman callers. She banked on the fact that they would be hotheaded, testosterone-fueled fools if someone upset her. So she held the stolen martini behind her back and made sure the stranger "bumped" right into her. She made a production out of him bumping her, and when the two men jumped to her defense, Sam slid into the empty booth, and while their attention was on the stranger, she placed the drugged martini under the table and stomped on it. When the two men were finally finished showing off their bravado, Sam downed the clean drink when they were watching and asked for more. They looked at each other with elation that Sam would soon be theirs for the taking.

While disgusted, Sam couldn't help but be glad the two men were such creeps. They would usher her right into the building she wanted to be in, and their guard would be so low, she would easily be able to incapacitate them before she went on the hunt for her friend Zhanna. And that was all that mattered. She just had to keep that in mind.

Over the last forty minutes, she had progressively acted more and more drunk, and though she didn't know what it felt like, she'd been trying to act drugged as well. Now that Patrick had arrived, she could really lay it on thick.

"You guyz er fun," Sam slurred. "I'm tired of thiz place." She drooped her eyes to feign drowsiness. "Canwego potty somewhere elze?" Sam laughed and slapped the guy beside her on the thigh. "Didyou hear that? I said potty"—she hiccupped—"but I meantosay party." She laughed and tipped her head back, then acted as if she was falling against the wall passed out.

"Sure. We have party back at our place."

Sam came back to life after his words. Her hair fell in front of her face. "Yes! That'swhatI'm talking about!"

The man beside her grabbed her around the waist and helped her out of the booth. Sam stumbled for effect. They caught her, and both of them helped her get her coat on, then led her out of the bar. It didn't take long for them to start groping her. Their needy hands roamed free all the way across the street. It was a good thing she'd moved her gun to the inside pocket of her coat, because if it were at the small of her back where she normally kept it, they would have found it a dozen times over in just a two-minute span.

Mercifully, they made it to the door of the closed deli. The man with the keys began unlocking the door, while the other pulled Sam close and tried to kiss her. She did her best to act as though she were passing out, but he was relentless. Thankfully the door was opened and she stumbled toward it to avoid his last attempt. Once inside, the man hit the light and a completely empty room appeared. Again, the attempts to kiss her came, and the other man pushed up behind her and began kissing her neck. The smell of vodka and bad cologne was enough to make her sick. She had to move this forward, or they were going to just go at her right there on the tile floor.

Sam pushed away long enough to get their attention. "I'mstill a lady, youknow," she continued to slur. "Take me to bed and bothofyou can have some fun."

Their faces both lit up, and the man in front yanked her by the hand to the back of the deli. They walked down a hallway, through a door, and out into a stairwell. They practically carried her up two flights of stairs, and their room was the first one they came to on the top floor. As one of them unlocked and opened the door, Sam stumbled inside. The place wasn't very big, and she walked backward toward the couch that was in the living room. She slid her coat off and tossed it on the floor. She curled her finger in a "come hither" fashion. And they practically came running.

Sam began lifting up her shirt. The first man made it to her and wrapped his arms around her waist. Kissing at her neck. The second man squeezed at her with his hands as he moved around behind her, pressing into her. She was elated that this disgusting farce was finally over.

Sam wrapped her hands around the man's neck in front of her and pulled his head back. He groaned with pleasure. As he went in for a kiss, she drove her right knee up into his groin with all the force she could muster. This time he grunted in pain. She spun around in a whip and brought a right elbow around with her. It connected to the side of the man's head and moved him back about a foot. She took advantage of the man being doubled over in front of her, and this time her knee blasted against his forehead. He fell backward onto the floor, unconscious.

"What the hell is wrong with you, bitch?" the man said as he rubbed his temple where the elbow had landed.

Sam really hated that word.

"I'm going to kill you, bitch!" he shouted.

She *really* hated it.

The man lunged at her, throwing a wild right hand at her face. Sam stepped to the side and kicked him in the stomach. His breath released, and he doubled over in pain. There was a lamp beside her that was begging for his head, so she obliged and crashed it over top of him. He dropped too. She wanted to kill them both, but she would have to wait for a more satisfactory revenge. This was about Zhanna.

She rummaged through a closet opposite the tiny kitchen and found some duct tape. She bound the men's hands and feet, placed a piece of tape over the mouths of both men, then pulled out her phone and called Patrick.

"Sam, you okay?"

"I'm fine. Come to the door of the deli on the corner across the street. I'll let you in. If Zhanna is here somewhere, we need to find her fast."

"On my way."

39

Barrow, Alaska, 2:53 p.m.

"Josiah! Do you hear me?!" King shouted again. Still no response.

There was a lot to juggle as he stood in the wrecked lobby of Volkov Mining—the room that had half a truck driven through it, dead bodies all around, and a deadly virus in a briefcase. On top of that, Josiah, King's escort out of there, wasn't responding after a truck had been coming his way outside, and he wanted to make sure Arnie got out of there alive as well. He couldn't worry about all of it, so he had to take it one step at a time.

"Arnie!"

The chubby security guard walked out of the break room into the lobby. His face was red, but it was eager.

"You and Roger take the back way out of here. Get home, and stay there. Don't worry about coming in for your shift tomorrow. No one will be working here for a while. Got it?"

"But what about the two—"

"Leave them. I have a team that will clean all this up. No more questions, just go. That's an order."

The official talk that he had used earlier with Arnie had worked, so he tried it again.

Arnie nodded, grabbed some keys from the desk, then left King and Kuznetsov alone in the lobby. That's when King heard gunshots through his earpiece, seemingly coming from outside the demolished front entrance.

"Stay close, but stay behind me. Got it?" he said to Kuznetsov.

Kuznetsov nodded. King went over to the desk and slid on his coat. The cold air was overtaking the warm lobby, and he knew outside was only going to be worse. He ejected the AR-15's magazine and gave it a look. There were still plenty of rounds inside. He locked it back in as he moved around the front of the truck stuck in the door space. Glass crunched beneath each step, and the frozen climate harshly welcomed him once he made it outside.

He and Kuznetsov were leaving a war zone. He'd hoped what lay ahead would be better, but the gunshots were still echoing near the gate, which he still couldn't see. The road wound around to his left, and it was just on the other side of some trees. He scanned the area around him; it seemed to be safe. He opened the back passenger door of Kuznetsov's SUV.

"Get in, and lie down in the back," King told him.

Kuznetsov did as he was told, climbed in, and lay down on the floor as King walked around the front and jumped in. Then King wheeled the SUV around and pointed toward the gate.

"Josiah!"

Nothing. The gunshots had stopped as well.

"Josiah, if you can hear me, I'm coming in the SUV. Be ready to jump in!"

King floored it, and gravel spun up beneath the tires. Gunshots rang out again in his ear. He wheeled around the turn, and the tall iron gates came into view. Both the exit and entrance gates were closed. But there were no trucks blocking the path. He could see two men standing behind a Humvee. The truck was off the road and low on one end; King supposed Josiah had managed to shoot out a tire. It was clear they were firing guns across the road as King drew closer; he just couldn't see what they were aiming at. All that mattered to him was that it wasn't Josiah and his man before he tried to stop them shooting by running right over them. And he could tell by the hats they were wearing that it wasn't.

King kept the pedal to the floor as the SUV approached the gate.

"Hold on to something, this is going to get rough!" King said to Kuznetsov.

King held the gas pedal down right through the gate. The crash was loud, and the thump of the iron gate against the front of the SUV jolted the entire vehicle. King's head bounced forward, but he managed to keep from connecting with the steering wheel. Immediately when the two men shooting from behind the Humvee heard the gate clash, they turned their guns toward King and the SUV. But it was too late. King was going almost seventy-five miles an hour.

The impact when he ran over the two men was big, but not nearly as wild as the crash against the gate.

As soon as King was past the Humvee, and the two men were roadkill, he slammed on the brakes and slid to a stop on the gravel. He opened the door and jumped out, his AR-15 in hand. He brought it to his shoulder and scanned the area. The two men had been shooting toward one of their own trucks. And just before King could call out, Josiah walked out from behind the truck with his hands up.

"X? Oh, thank God. I thought I was a dead man!"

King lowered his gun and walked over to Josiah. He had blood all over him. "You hurt?"

"No, but Jerry . . ." Josiah looked back over his shoulder while shaking his head. "He got hit. I tried to keep the blood inside him. I just couldn't. It was awful."

Josiah was starting to get emotional. King could certainly feel his pain. He'd lost many friends over the years, but he was already focused forward, and they needed to get moving.

"I'm sorry, Josiah. But Cali is in danger. We have to go."

Josiah's eyes widened. He was hurting, but he didn't want something to happen to Cali or his other two men at the airport.

Then they heard gravel being kicked up in the distance. Someone else was coming.

"Shit!" King said. "Let's go. Now! You drive, I'll shoot!"

He and Josiah raced to the SUV and jumped inside. King rolled down the window as Josiah put the car in drive and took off. King fully expected to see another Humvee rounding the corner. His plan was to shoot the driver's side of the front windshield as soon as it came into view. He reached the gun out the window into the freezing cold air, but his adrenaline kept his body from registering the cold. He wrapped his finger around the trigger and readied himself.

"It's my guys," Josiah said. "Hold your fire, it's my guys!"

King immediately brought the gun back inside and rolled up the window. An old Ford Bronco came racing around the curve. Josiah flashed his lights, and they both slowed to a stop and rolled the windows down.

"Follow me to the airport. We have to hurry!" Josiah shouted.

The Bronco whipped around and fell in behind their SUV.

"How the hell did you get out of there alive? I lost my earpiece when I dove for cover. I thought for sure you were a goner. Sorry I couldn't help."

"I had some help from another security guard. And I'd figured your earpiece came unplugged. I'm just glad I made it to you before those men advanced on you."

"Poor Jerry. He was such a good guy, man."

King was quiet. Experience told him no words could help, so he didn't waste any. Instead he focused on the airport. If they could get out of there with their lives, he had to get to Moscow as fast as he could. But he didn't know what to do with Kuznetsov and his briefcase package worth about a million deaths or more. He couldn't leave him in Barrow, but if he took Kuznetsov along with him, he would drag King down. King needed to get to Sam as fast as possible, and he knew even that might be too late.

<<<<>>>>

40

BEFORE SAM LEFT the apartment where she'd tied up the two men who'd tried to drug her at the bar, she took her gun from her coat, turned the television on, and hiked up the volume. The apartment complex was quiet, and even though she'd taped their mouths, the men groaning to be freed after being beaten up by a girl would have been loud enough for someone to hear. And because Sam hoped Zhanna was somewhere in that building, she figured someone was probably awake and standing guard. The last thing she wanted to do was alert whoever that might be.

She slinked down the stairs and back into the deli. The keys she took from Romeo number one upstairs unlocked the interior door. She went to the front door and let agent O'Connor inside. He was wide-eyed as he stepped in, and his hand was at the small of his back in case he needed his gun.

"It's all right, I have them tied up."

Patrick relaxed. "How'd you manage that?"

"I could have managed that even if I had actually been drugged. They weren't exactly trained killers."

Patrick looked impressed. "So, what now? Are these two guys even involved with why we're here?"

"I honestly don't know," Sam said.

"You going to question them?"

Sam didn't answer. She looked around the empty room. There was literally nothing but tile and empty walls. She walked over to an open doorway. It led to the kitchen. There wasn't any equipment left, but there was a bright red lever on the wall with the word FIRE etched in white. Patrick walked in behind her. She looked up at him with a raised eyebrow.

"Might actually work," he said.

The trouble with it as Sam saw it was that even if someone was holding Zhanna hostage in that apartment complex, they couldn't let her outside bound and gagged. Everyone would see. So they would most likely just keep Zhanna in the room while they went out to investigate if there was an actual threat of fire. Sam was sure she would be able to tell if someone was investigating in such a way. They would have a different look than the other dwellers who would be forced outside. For one, they would be fully clothed, not dressed in any sort of sleepwear. But even if multiple people actually took the time to dress, whoever was holding Zhanna would still have a more investigative vibe.

"I think it's worth a shot," Patrick said. "Let's split up and see if we can find someone who comes out looking suspicious."

"You know that's a federal offense, pulling a fire alarm without cause."

Patrick laughed. "Maybe you can get the president to get Putin to pardon me since y'all are buddies."

Sam shrugged. Patrick walked over and pulled the fire alarm. A loud bell began ringing immediately. He and Sam rushed out the deli door. She pointed for him to go around front, and she went left around the back. Sam was cold without her coat, but she was determined. As people started filing out of the complex, she wrapped her arms around herself and searched each and every person. Couples, singles, old, and young continued out, all wearing the same sleepy but worried expression. Only a few people were fully dressed, and they were all young, still holding their drinks. There was no one behind the building who gave Sam the impression they were the person she was looking for. After a few moments of no one else exiting the building, she went around front.

She passed the deli door, and as soon as she rounded the corner, she noticed Patrick towering above the small crowd of people. He was a big guy, so it wasn't hard. She also watched as he stared intently at something; clearly he'd found something to focus on. Finally, he looked over at her, then gave a nod of his head ahead of him. Sam looked that way and found a man with a black leather jacket pacing back and forth as he searched the crowd. As Sam started to move in his direction, she noticed a man with a set of keys walking her way. She didn't know a lot about fires, but she did know that to stop the fire alarm from sounding, you had to have a key. If this man happened to be maintenance for the building, he might be walking to turn it off. If he did, it was the perfect scenario. It would keep the police from coming, and because the alarm was off, residents would be going back inside, which would give her and Patrick the opportunity to follow the man in the leather jacket back to whatever apartment he came from.

The man with the keys walked by her and opened the deli door. Sam waited and watched the man who was still searching the crowd for a reason to be nervous. Maybe that was what he was doing. Sam didn't have any real evidence he was involved with anything at that point. Just a hunch.

Finally, the ringing alarm went silent. A roar of applause from the cold residents sounded, and the man in the leather jacket began walking toward the main entrance at the middle of the building. Sam quickly stepped his way, avoiding people as best she could. Luckily, Patrick had moved in right behind him, and she couldn't possibly lose sight of him as he was at least a head taller than everyone else.

She stayed close as they moved up the stairs. Everyone seemed convinced there was no fire. Lack of smoke and the alarm stopping had satisfied their fears. As they reached the top floor—the same floor Sam had subdued the other men —Leather Man stopped at a door and placed his key in the lock. Patrick kept casually strolling by. Leather Man looked her way, but there was another couple in between them. Then she watched as Leather Man stopped trying to unlock his door, and he reached for the small of his back.

Sam couldn't shoot him. She had no real idea who he was or what he was doing. All she could think to do was pull her gun and shout at him.

"Freeze! Police!"

Leather Man wheeled around and put his hands in the air. He didn't have a gun in his hand. Patrick turned around and rushed up behind him, taking his hands down and holding them behind his back. He shouted something in Russian at Sam. Sam just walked forward and unlocked the door. Leather Man had a pleading tone, but Sam couldn't understand him. She pushed his door inward and held up her gun. She didn't know what she expected to find, but there was no Zhanna tied to a chair like she'd hoped. All of them moved inside the apartment.

"I thought he was reaching for a gun," Sam said to Patrick. "He put his hand behind his back while he was unlocking the door."

Patrick carried him over to the sofa in the middle of the room, bent him over it, and reached for the small of Leather Man's back. Leather Man shouted again. Patrick pulled out a bag of something white.

"No gun," Patrick said. "But here's why he looked paranoid."

Sam hung her head and put away her gun. She knew he'd looked suspicious, but it wasn't for the reason she'd hoped.

Patrick let the man go, and he ran to the other side of the room, begging in his native tongue. Patrick tossed down the bag of cocaine and turned to Sam. "You didn't really think they'd be dumb enough to keep your girl here where they told you to meet, did you?'

"Wishful thinking is a powerful thing."

"So you think those guys you tied up are just a couple of creeps?"

"Guys?" Sam hadn't given the two men she had duct taped together a second thought. "The guys!"

Sam bolted out of the man's apartment. As soon as she hit the hallway, a man was walking into the apartment at the end of the hall where she'd left the two men. She motioned Patrick forward as she raced down the hallway to the door. She heard a man's voice say something in Russian, his tone sounding surprised. Sam nodded to Patrick who was now holding his own gun, and she turned the corner. The man who Sam had seen walk in before them was bent over the subdued men, and had just removed the first guy's duct tape from his mouth. The man who'd been groping her not long ago nodded in Sam's direction and shouted something. The man trying to free them looked up and started reaching for his gun. But he stopped and froze with a surprised look on his face. Sam thought it was because she was already holding her gun on him. Then she heard Patrick behind her.

"Agent Huang? What the hell are you doing here, Vince?"

41

President Gibbons paced laps around his desk in the Oval Office. He hadn't received an update from Director Lucas in almost an hour. Nothing about Warshaw, nothing about Sam, and nothing about Alexander King. If patience was a virtue, he was lacking. He couldn't stand not knowing what was going on. He had some devastating decisions to make, and he needed to know more before he could make a move. He was ready to send a team to strike down Volkov Mining in Barrow. He was ready to ground Nigel Warshaw, regardless of political backlash if Warshaw had no involvement. And he was a knuckle hair away from waking up the Russian government to get answers for everything their people seemed to be sticking their noses into.

"Here, honey, you have got to calm down."

Gibbons jumped when he heard his wife's voice. He was so much inside his own head he hadn't even noticed her walk in. She wore a pitying grin as she reached a glass toward him.

"Sorry, I'm in my own world here," he said as he walked over, kissed her on the cheek, and took the glass. He could tell by the sweet aroma that it was bourbon. Normally he was a scotch guy, but ever since the meeting with King a few weeks ago when they'd shared some of Kentucky's finest, he'd been on a bourbon kick. The hardest part was not overdoing it as he dealt with all the world's problems.

"It's all right." Beth rubbed his arm as she tried to console him. "I just thought you could probably use a drink. Everything's going to be all right, you know? You have the best on it. And you have the American people's best interest at heart."

"Yeah, but you know what they say. The path to hell is paved with good intentions."

She patted him on the arm and turned to walk away. "Just don't go cynical on me, okay?"

He gave her a nod. "Thanks for the drink, sweetheart." After his first two weeks on the job, he couldn't imagine a president could be anything but cynical after being in office.

Finally, his phone began ringing. When he saw it was Director Lucas, he took the bourbon down in one slug and answered. "Talk to me."

"It was smoke and mirrors."

"Kuznetsov?" the president said.

"No, Warshaw having his pilot go to the airport. And the car they left in from Warshaw's house."

"Break it down for me, Robert."

"Warshaw wasn't in the car we thought he took to the airport where his plane and his pilot are. When the SUV got to the airport, it was only the driver inside."

"So now that your agent approached the empty SUV, his driver definitely called Warshaw and tipped him off. Now Warshaw knows we are watching him. Damn it!"

"Sir, he clearly already knew. He played my agent because of it."

"So where is he now? We have reason enough to detain him now, right?'

"If we didn't because of that, we do for another reason," Lucas said.

"Well?"

"We've been combing his accounts. We found two large bank transfers to a medical company in China. We've got him dead to rights."

"Not if we don't know where he is. Don't let him leave this country, Robert. You hear me?'

"We're on it."

Gibbons rubbed his eyes at the bridge of his nose with his thumb and index finger. He couldn't believe what was happening. "Anything from Sam Harrison or King?"

"Just got off the phone with King. That's what took me so long to call. He's okay. And he has Kuznetsov and samples of both the virus and the vaccine with him."

"Wow. This is huge, right?"

"It's hopeful," Director Lucas said. "We don't know for certain if there aren't more samples like the ones that showed up in Moscow floating around. And King says Kuznetsov claims to have nothing to do with weaponizing a virus. He wants to know what to do with Kuznetsov and the samples."

"Does King think Kuznetsov is telling the truth?"

"He doesn't know what to believe."

Gibbons was about to respond when his secretary interrupted by calling in.

"Hold on, Robert." He pressed the button for the other line. "I'm busy, Allison, hold my calls."

"Sir, it's someone saying it's extremely urgent. Says you call him X?"

Gibbons didn't know why, but hearing that King was calling him directly and not going through Robert made his spine tingle. "All right. Put him through."

Gibbons switched back to Director Lucas. "I'll call you right back, something came up."

He didn't wait for a response. Gibbons clicked the blinking light on the phone. "X? This really you?"

"Sorry to call you direct, but I don't have a choice."

"Well, shit, out with it already. You all right?"

"Can I speak freely?"

Gibbons didn't like that question. "Uh oh. Of course, son."

Then King shocked him. "Do you trust Director Lucas?"

Gibbons had no idea how to answer that question. His knee-jerk reaction was to say of course, but he knew if King was asking, there must be a reason. "Do I have a reason not to?"

"I don't know, but we have to find out. I need to know where Lucas was on the evening of August 3 last year. If you can tell me that, I can tell you if we can trust him."

"I don't like this, X. This is your superior."

"Do you trust me?" King said.

There was no hesitation. "You know I do. You've proved your loyalty."

"Then find out where Lucas was on August 3 as soon as possible. For now, I have to figure out what the hell to do next. I'm out here with no one to trust. I have no idea who is involved with this mess, and my partner in crime is fighting for her life in Moscow. I need some hard answers or this thing is going to get away from us, sir."

"Say no more," the president said. "I'll call you back as soon as I can. What are you going to do with Kuznetsov and the samples?"

Gibbons heard King let out a sigh. "Good question."

42

King ended the call with the president. He didn't want to go over Director Lucas's head, but he didn't have a choice. He needed to make some progress on what was happening.

King, Josiah, and Kuznetsov were only a couple of minutes from the airport. The snow had almost come to a complete stop, giving King hope that Cali could fly them out of there. Josiah had radioed ahead to his men there to let Cali know to get the plane ready. Josiah didn't say anything after that; he was probably in shock after losing his friend. And Kuznetsov's mind was most likely too blown to speak after the carnage he'd just witnessed. So all were silent on the ride through the dying twilight.

The quiet time gave King a chance to organize his thoughts. There were several things that needed to be addressed, not the least of which was where he was going to tell Cali to fly. But the first thing burning in his head wasn't where but who. According to everything that Kuznetsov was saying, it was the US government that was responsible for hiring him to work on the virus. If that was actually the case, the president had no idea, or he would have told King when he asked about Director Lucas. But what did that mean when the president didn't say the US *was* responsible? Did it mean Lucas actually was the one pulling the strings? Did it mean Kuznetsov was lying about everything? Or did it mean someone like Nigel Warshaw had fooled Kuznetsov into believing he was working for the United States in order to keep everything quiet?

The key to some of that entire mess was if Director Lucas was actually in Seattle and if he really did meet with Kuznetsov. Hopefully President Gibbons could shine some light on that. However, King had to figure out what to do until then. If he left for Moscow now, he still wouldn't make it in time to help Sam. Not unless he could charter a plane from Anchorage that would be waiting to fly him through the night. That was a possible option. But what about Kuznetsov? And what about the man who'd been flying to the nearby towns and releasing the virus? Could he be the quickest route to finding out who was really behind this entire operation?

"Kuznetsov," King said, breaking the silence in the truck. "You said the same man had left the lab with samples each time you saw them go. Who was he, and where did he go last?"

"His name is Vince Huang. He—"

"He's Asian?"

"Chinese American I believe," Kuznetsov said. "Never got too friendly with anyone. But that is the nature of his work."

"What do you mean by 'the nature of his work'?"

"Like you, I have no idea what his true identity is."

King was confused. "You mean he is an American operative?"

"That's what I was told, but it seems I have been lied to often over the past six months."

"Okay, so you were told this Vince Huang works for the CIA?" King said.

"He is who I report through. My liaison, if you will."

"But you said there were three scientists working with you." Something wasn't adding up for King. This was really the first time he'd found a flaw in Kuznetsov's story. "You didn't say anything about a CIA man there with you. And I certainly don't know of one who was supposed to be there. Why didn't you mention him before?'

"Because how do I know I can trust you?" Kuznetsov was getting defensive. "No one from US government told me you were coming here. Someone is lying to you."

King turned around in his seat and looked Kuznetsov in the eyes. "No shit someone is lying to me. I'm just trying to figure out if that someone is you."

Josiah interrupted the staring contest. "We're right around the corner, X. What do you want to do?"

King was quiet. He had some big decisions to make, and he had to make them a lot quicker than he wanted and with a lot less information than he needed. He had to handle what was in front of him first, before he could move on to anything else. And the closest thing he could have an effect on was running down this Vince Huang. If King could make him talk, the pieces of the puzzle might come together a whole lot faster.

"X?" Josiah prompted.

"I need your help," King said.

"I'm here. What do you need?"

"I can't take Kuznetsov with me. So I need you to watch him for me."

"Okay, done." Josiah was eager.

"But I don't know who might come looking for him, so it might put you in danger."

"You mean more than I already have been?" Josiah laughed as he put on his turn signal. The airport was just ahead on the left.

"Maybe. I have no idea really."

Kuznetsov spoke up. "You think people want me?"

King turned and pointed to the floor of the SUV. "I know they want what's in that briefcase. That's enough for me."

"Then you must take me with you. I am not safe here."

"I can't do that. But there's one place I think you will be safe."

"Where? They'll find me!" Kuznetsov was frightened.

"I'm not taking him to my house," Josiah said. "I have a kid. I can't put her in danger."

"Not your house, Josiah. You're going to take him to jail."

Needless to say, Kuznetsov was not happy. Josiah turned into the airport to a chorus of screaming and shouting by Kuznetsov.

"I am a world-renowned scientist! And I've done nothing wrong. I will not sit in a prison cell!"

"Would you rather die?" King said. "Because that is a real possibility."

That shut Kuznetsov up. Josiah passed through the security gate and drove right over to Cali's dad's plane. It was a King Air, and the props were already turning.

Now King just needed to decide where he was going. Atqasuk seemed to be the only logical place if that's where the supposed American operative went. He pulled out his phone and dialed Dbie.

"I'm sorry, X," Dbie answered. "I don't have anything yet."

King bypassed her apology. "I need everything there is to know about a Vince Huang. And I need it STAT."

"So this is my new priority?"

"It's your only priority, Dbie."

"You got it. Just so I have a direction, does it have anything to do with Nigel Warshaw whom you also have me looking into?"

King hadn't thought about it, but if Kuznetsov was lying, and maybe working for Warshaw, the two could absolutely be connected. "Could be. Not sure, but run it down."

"Will do. I'll call back as soon as I have anything for you."

King got out of the SUV, but not before he took the briefcase from the back.

"You can't take that!" Kuznetsov shouted.

"I'm not leaving this with you. Just lay low, hopefully I won't be long."

Kuznetsov banged the seat in front of him. King walked around to Josiah who had also gotten out.

"I'll make sure he is safe," Josiah shouted over the sound of the propellers.

"Thanks, Josiah. For everything. Sorry about your friend."

Josiah nodded, then shook King's hand. "Go stop whoever is doing this. That's all I ask. Then his death will mean something at least."

"I'll do everything I can."

Josiah let go of his hand, and when King turned away, he saw Cali coming. All he could see were her eyes; she was so bundled up, she looked like she was getting ready for night skiing. But so did everyone else in that frozen town.

She ran up and wrapped her arms around him. "The guys told me it was bad!" she shouted. "I'm glad you're okay! Where we headed?"

"Atqasuk!" he shouted. The plane was even louder as they approached the door.

Her face slumped. "Sorry, I can't take you there! The snow storm has it all covered up!"

43

Moscow, Russia, 1:55 a.m.

Sam looked back at Patrick in shock. "You know him?"

The two men taped together on the floor had the same look Sam did, only they were looking at the man trying to free them.

"What the hell is going on?" Patrick said.

Sam didn't lower her weapon. Vince Huang didn't say a word. Below his black spiky hair his very soft Asian features wore a worried look. No one knew who was going to break the silence first.

Sam was quiet long enough. She had a friend to save. "Well, if no one wants to talk, then I'll just start shooting. Your choice."

"How you know these people?" the Russian man without the duct tape on his mouth said to Vince.

Vince replaced the duct tape, then walked toward Sam.

"Not another step."

Vince put up his hands. "Look, I'm on your team. Can we go out in the hall and talk?"

Sam looked back at Patrick. Patrick nodded. The three of them went back out the door to a chorus of grunts and groans from the subdued men.

"What the hell is going on?" Patrick said to Vince.

"They are my informants. I stopped by after something went down at the airport earlier to see if they knew anything."

"Informants?" Sam said. She turned to Patrick. "Who the hell is he?"

"When I first got with the FBI several years ago, Vince and I worked a few cases together."

"So you're FBI?" Sam asked Vince.

"Yes. We are investigating a human trafficking ring involving a lot of US citizens. We are about to bring one of the big ones down. Please don't mess this up for me."

She had no trouble believing the two creeps could be involved in a human trafficking ring. However, what this Vince Huang didn't know was that Sam was involved in the something that went wrong at the airport, and it didn't have a thing to do with human trafficking. But for the time being, she kept her mouth shut. She needed to get Patrick alone to see what kind of guy Vince was.

"We certainly don't want to mess up a trafficking investigation," Sam said. "If they are your informants, just let them know that we were hired privately and that you took care of it. If this is all about human trafficking, we were wrong to be here anyway."

"Why are you here?" Vince asked Patrick.

"We really can't—"

"Someone kidnapped an asset," Sam interrupted

Patrick. "We were already here on assignment, so they put us on it. I'm so glad you've heard about the mess at the airport. That is where our asset was taken. Any information you could give us would be unbelievably helpful. And we'll be out of your hair."

Sam could tell by the pretend dumbfounded look on his face that he knew exactly what she was talking about. The question was, why was he lying?

"Let-Let me just go back in here and smooth this over with these guys. Then I'll see what I can find out about your asset."

"That would be great. Thank you so much!" Sam said. The cheer in her own voice made her stomach turn, but Vince believed it enough to go back inside the apartment.

Sam turned immediately and yanked Patrick in the opposite direction down the hallway. "Who the hell is he, Patrick? Because he is lying through his teeth."

"I thought the same thing. How could he know about the airport? I never did really like the guy, but I just thought it was because he was an arrogant prick."

Sam thought for a moment. She needed answers, and fast. This guy was lying about something. She pulled out her phone and dialed Director Lucas. The phone rang several times, then went to voice mail. "Shit!" She then dialed the only other person she thought could find some info on Vince in a relatively short time period: Dbie Johnson. Dbie picked up on the first ring.

"Busy night," Dbie answered.

"I'm sorry?"

"Oh, nothing. X just called, so I was saying—"

"Is he all right?"

"Just looking for information."

"Well, I need you to do something for me first," Sam said.

"I'll do what I can. What is it?"

"I need anything you can find out about a Vince Huang."

Dbie laughed. "Yeah, I know. I'm on it."

"What?"

"You talked to X too?" Dbie said.

"Dbie, what are you saying? I haven't spoken with anyone."

"You're kidding?"

"I don't have time for whatever this is. There are lives at stake."

"Shit, you're serious," Dbie said, changing her tone. "I swear to God I just got off the phone with X and he asked for information about the same guy."

"He asked about Vince Huang?"

"Yes, crazy, right?"

"Get the information, I'll call you back." Sam ended the call.

"Everything all right?" Patrick said.

"No, your man in there—"

Sam didn't get a chance to finish. Patrick grabbed her by the shirt, lowered his shoulder into the door beside him, crashing through it and pulling her in with him. The reason he had done so echoed through the hallway: someone had just about shot Sam in the back.

Sam jumped up to her feet. As if knowing that Xander was looking for the same guy wasn't enough to let her know she couldn't let Vince get away, now he'd shot at her. The building was about to turn into chaos. Sam could hear people screaming in their apartments. Luckily, no one seemed to be home in the one they'd just crashed into.

"He can't get away," Sam said to Patrick. "You go left, I'll follow directly after them."

Patrick didn't argue. He jumped up and filed in behind Sam. Sam poked her head out and nearly lost it. Vince was firing on her one last time before he disappeared into the stairwell.

"Go, go, go!" Sam shouted as she sprinted down the hallway. What might be the key to pulling all of this together was getting away. At the very least, she knew Vince would know how to find Zhanna. If Xander was looking for Vince too, it meant what happened at the airport had to be somehow connected to something Xander had found in Alaska. She raced down the stairs, dodging a few screaming civilians as she went.

Sam would die before she let him get away.

44

SAM JUMPED THE LAST SIX STEPS AND SKIDDED TO A STOP ON the tile floor. She pushed through the door that led into the deli. As soon as she cleared it, she was hit hard from behind. As she slid across the floor, she spun into her attacker. It was Vince, and he was already on top of her. As Sam wrapped her legs around him and pulled guard so he couldn't raise up and hit her, they both heard gunshots outside and whipped their heads toward the door. Shouting followed outside, then more gunshots. It was dark outside, and dark in that room. She hoped Patrick was okay.

Vince struggled inside Sam's guard. He tried to buck upward to free himself, but she held on tight with her arms and legs wrapped around him.

"Who are you?" Sam grunted.

Vince answered by lifting her all the way up until he was standing. He was going to slam her on her back if she didn't let go. When he started his motion downward, she released him and pushed herself back. Two feet of separation had him reaching for his gun. Sam rushed forward and dove at his legs. Vince kicked them back and sprawled away from her. He clearly had Jiu Jitsu training. He landed on top of her and was forcing his hips down as he wrapped his arm around her neck. She was in a bad position, but at least she wasn't staring down the barrel of his gun.

There was only so long she was going to be able to keep him from getting the best of her. Jiu Jitsu is a great equalizer if strength is unmatched. It gave a woman a fighting chance against a man twice her size. But when Jiu Jitsu skills are equal, the stronger of the two would eventually win. Unless he got tired.

Sam shot her hand in between his arm and her neck, giving her a chance to fight the choke he was attempting. She felt the stitches in her shoulder rip apart. His squeeze was powerful. He was stronger than his wiry frame suggested. She did the only thing she could do and reached for his groin. She grabbed enough of it that her squeeze weakened his hold, and he let out a moan of pain.

Finally, he was forced to let go. They both separated. He threw a quick right hand that Sam was able to slip, but the left hook that followed hit her right in the kidney. Pain flooded her system, and she couldn't defend against the overhand right he followed with, which smacked her in the forehead. She saw purple stars as she felt her ass hit the floor. She was disoriented, but she could still see that he was coming for her. She tried to get up, but she couldn't. Her brain wasn't firing fast enough to tell her arms what she wanted them to. She was in trouble.

The next thing she knew, there was a massive crash at the deli's front door, then a large shadow flashed through the room. Sam thought she might have been hallucinating until she heard a grunt, and Vince's figure disappeared in front of her. She shook her head to clear the cobwebs, and when her wits finally returned, she saw the grizzly bear she'd been hoping for on top of Vince. Patrick was beating him to death.

Sam ran over and tried to pull Patrick back by his shoulders, but it was like trying to pull a truck that was in park. He only rocked back slightly, but she couldn't budge him. She could see by some of the yellow streetlight flooding in through the cracks in the boarded windows that Vince was limp beneath him.

"Patrick, stop! Don't kill him! We need information!"

She tried to pull at him again, but he was in a raged trance. Finally, she circled around and slapped him hard in the face. "Patrick, stop!" Then she shoved him, and he finally fell back. "I need him to tell me where Zhanna is!"

Patrick shook his head and stood up. They both looked down at Vince. He wasn't moving. Sam pushed Patrick aside and knelt beside Vince. "Vince! Wake up." She shook him a little. "Wake up!" She stood back up, and when she looked at Patrick, he began pacing and nervously running his fingers through his hair.

"I'm sorry. I-I saw him hit you—"

Finally, Vince coughed up blood and moaned a desperate sigh. Patrick stopped pacing, and the look on his face was of great relief. He was more calm this time.

"Sam, I'm sorry. I just—when I saw him hit you, I lost it!"

Completely out of character, Sam rushed over and wrapped her arms around him. The grizzly bear gave her a bear hug.

"Thank you."

There was little doubt in Sam's mind that she would

have died if Patrick hadn't been there. Patrick just kept squeezing. Finally, Sam came to her senses and wiggled out from his arms. "Now you just have to learn to control yourself. Christ, you're like an animal."

Patrick shrugged.

Sam pointed toward the door. "What about those two?"

"They weren't very good shots."

"We need to go. Can you go get your car and pull over here? We can put him in the back."

As Patrick was walking out the door, Sam's phone began to vibrate in her pocket. She was in no danger from Vince. He still had no idea where he was.

"Hello?" When Sam answered, she could hear a loud engine. Sounded like the propellers of a plane.

"Sam, it's X. You all right? I just talked to Dbie again, and she said you were asking about Vince Huang too?"

"I'm okay. Vince, however, isn't doing so well."

"You have him?" King's voice was filled with excitement.

"I do. Where are you?"

"Hang on, Sam." King's voice went muffled, but she could still hear him. "Turn around, we don't need to go. We've got him." Then he came back to the phone. "Damn, I'm glad I called. I was getting ready to fly to a town just south of here to try to find him. What the hell is he doing in Moscow, and who the hell is he?"

"Both good questions. Haven't made it that far with him yet. It's been a bit of a fight."

"What about Zhanna?"

"Nothing yet. Vince is regaining consciousness. I'll torture it out of him if I have to."

"So you think he knows where she is?" The propeller sound surrounding King's voice had lessened.

"I have no idea. What do you know about him? What's going on in Barrow?"

"I have Kuznetsov."

Sam smiled. Of course he did.

"And I have the last of the virus and vaccine that was left here. Kuznetsov claims that Director Lucas personally met with him and brought him on to find a cure for the virus for the US government."

Sam actually laughed. "Did you let him live?"

"I did, because I don't know what to believe." King's voice returned to normal as the propellers shut down. "Kuznetsov said the day he was at the World Health Conference, Nigel Warshaw brokered a meeting with Director Lucas. Said he met with him right there and that they paid him a bunch of money to create a vaccine for this virus that no one knows about."

"And you couldn't ask Director Lucas about it, because of course he would say he wasn't involved," Sam said knowingly.

"Right," King said. "Because if the US government was involved, President Gibbons wouldn't have sent us in. So either Lucas is involved without the president knowing, or Kuznetsov is full of shit. But I still don't have an answer."

"Where does Vince Huang fit in?"

Right then, Patrick came busting through the door. "We gotta go. Sirens are blaring."

Sam nodded and walked to the door. Patrick picked Vince up and slung him over his shoulder. When Sam stepped out into the cold, she, too, could hear the sirens. There were two dead bodies lying in the street, and some people were gathered around to watch.

King answered her question as Sam moved toward

Patrick's running sedan. "Kuznetsov said Vince was his liaison between Kuznetsov and the US government. Said he was the guy taking the samples out of the lab each time the small Alaskan towns were getting sick. The timing lined up—"

"That's why you thought Kuznetsov might be telling the truth," Sam said. "I get it. But Vince is here in Moscow with me. So what now?"

"It at least shows that Barrow is connected to Moscow," King said. "It's who's really moving the chess pieces that we don't know. I asked the president to find out on the low if Director Lucas was in Seattle when Kuznetsov says the meeting between them happened. That will help us scratch Lucas off the list. Then, the only other common denominator is—"

"Nigel Warshaw," Sam finished his sentence. She got in the car and watched Patrick stuff a still dazed Vince Huang in the back seat.

"Exactly—"

"Hold on, X. Dbie is calling. I'll patch her in."

Sam answered the call and hit the button to merge them together. "Dbie, you are on with me and X. Tell us what you've got."

"A lot actually," Dbie said.

"Fire away," King said.

"Want me to start with Nigel Warshaw? Or Vince Huang?"

Both Sam and King said "Warshaw" at the same time. Patrick got in the car and sped out of the apartment complex's parking lot. The police couldn't have been more than a few blocks away.

"Okay," Dbie said, clearing her throat, "the reason it

took me so long to get info on Warshaw was because I had to find a back way into his bank accounts. There are a lot of rumors on the dark web, and the internet, for that matter, about him investing in vaccine companies and so forth, but all of the holding companies I found of his were all dead ends. So I thought going straight to the money was the fastest route."

"We don't have a lot of time here, Dbie. Can you keep it short?"

"Yes. Warshaw wired two multimillion-dollar amounts to the same hospital in China. Both through a couple of different Cayman and Swedish accounts. The hospital he sent the money to specializes in viruses, among other things."

"So it's Warshaw?" King said.

"Certainly sounds that way," Sam said. Patrick jerked the car around a few turns, then pulled to a stop under a dark bridge. "X, you think the money he wired to China was to build the virus? Then everything in Barrow was done for the vaccine?"

"Makes sense with Warshaw's narrative to the media," King said. "He's been preaching mandatory vaccinations for years."

Sam got out of the car. "And you think this was his way of making sure he set the precedent? Created a virus so deadly and so contagious that it forced the government's hand to mandate?"

"The pieces certainly fit. Anything out of Vince yet?"

"Just about to find out," Sam said. "Dbie, what did you find on him?"

"He was former FBI. Had a falling out and they let him go. Killed someone who didn't give him information or something. It's a muddy case that was classified. That was several years ago. Hasn't been employed on record since."

King spoke up. "There's his motive to work on something like this. It fits what we are finding. Warshaw probably sought him out to pose as a CIA agent to Kuznetsov. He could play the part because he'd actually been a federal agent."

"So does that mean you think Kuznetsov is innocent in all of this?" Sam said.

"Every part of his story lines up," King said. "Looks like Warshaw pulled one over on him. Made him believe it really was Director Lucas that he met with, and that it was the US government that wanted the vaccine."

Patrick had already pulled Vince out the back of the car and was questioning him.

"I've got to go," Sam said. "I'll have an update on Vince in a few. X, can you call Lucas and have him corroborate what we've found? Then he can send a team to go get Warshaw before he slips away?"

"On it. Then I'm getting the hell out of this frozen tundra."

"Meet you on the beach?" Sam said.

"Ooh, ooh. Take me!" Dbie chimed in.

"Meet you both there. Sam, you bring Zhanna, will you?"

"Working on that right now."

45

President Gibbons put down his fork and pushed the plate away. He had only taken one bite. The ribeye was delicious, but he didn't have the stomach for it. His stomach was too busy tying up in knots waiting for Director Lucas to get back to him. If Warshaw made it out of the country, it could be a real problem running him down. Not to mention how hard it would be to stop anyone from bringing the virus to the continental US. So much was riding on this that he couldn't even sit still.

As soon as he stood from the table in the Oval Office, the phone on his desk rang. He practically sprinted over to it. "Yes?"

"Mr. President," his secretary said. His shoulders slumped because Director Lucas would have called the direct line.

"Yes, Allison?"

"It's General Davis on the line for you."

He perked back up. He'd tasked the general with finding out where Director Lucas was on August 3 of last year like King had asked him to do.

"Put him through."

Since he'd gotten off the phone with King, Director Lucas hadn't called Gibbons back. He couldn't keep his mind from wandering down the path that if Lucas was involved, maybe he was taking this time to leave the country too. Maybe he said he didn't find Warshaw at the airport because he was covering for him. If idle hands are the devil's tools, then an idle mind is the devil's playground. And Gibbons's thoughts were definitely on Satan's seesaw.

"Mr. President?"

"Yes, General, what did you find?" President Gibbons held his breath.

"We combed through the CIA travel log and the key card logs at Langley. Director Lucas was in his office until almost eight o'clock the night of August 3."

"You're certain of this?"

"Yes, sir. His security badge logged him in that morning and out that evening. And we went back and double-checked the video footage there too. He was there. No way he was in Seattle, Washington."

The president let out a sigh of relief. He had enough people coming after him and lying to him. The last thing he needed was the director of the CIA being one of them.

"Thank you, General. This was a tremendous help."

"No problem, sir."

"I'll be in touch."

Gibbons ended the call. Now he just needed to hear from Lucas about Warshaw. The more information they'd gathered about Warshaw, the more suspicious he looked. But just like with Director Lucas, Gibbons was doing his best not to jump to conclusions. Then his phone rang again. He answered it before the first ring finished.

"The man calling himself X, for you again," Allison said.

"Put him through."

"You there, sir?"

"Go ahead, King."

"We're nearly certain it was Warshaw. Please tell me you have him in custody?" King said.

"I'm still waiting on word."

"Shit."

"I know, but I do have good news," Gibbons said.

"I'll take all of that I can get."

"Director Lucas was at Langley all day on the third of August. Video evidence. No way he met with Kuznetsov."

"I figured. Good to know. So either Warshaw or Kuznetsov is lying."

"And you think it's Warshaw?" Gibbons said.

"We do. I just spoke with Sam. She found one of his men who's been posing as CIA for Kuznetsov. He'd been in Barrow, but ended up getting into it with Sam in Moscow. So obviously it's connected."

"What's the endgame?"

"Money and power," King said. "Same as most endgames, I guess. Warshaw has been pushing for mandatory vaccines, and this was his way to get it. Create a virus *and* the vaccine."

"That's what the large sums of money to China were for, you think?"

"If he's not guilty, it's the biggest coincidence in the history of mankind."

Gibbons's phone rang again. "Gotta run, hopefully this is Lucas. I'll get right back to you." He pressed the other line. "Go ahead."

"It's Robert."

Gibbons stood from his seat. This was it. Director Lucas finally called him back.

"You got Warshaw?"

"We got him, sir."

Gibbons smacked his hand on the desk in celebration. "Hell yeah!"

"But sir?"

Shit. This was not a good time for buts. "Uh oh."

"Warshaw's not involved with this virus. He doesn't have anything to do with what's going on in Alaska and Russia. It was all a huge coincidence."

"How . . . How could you possibly know that already?"

"Our guys caught up to him right after I got off the phone with you. I've spent the last hour sorting it all out and double-checking his story. It's solid."

"Well, spit it out. I need to get word back to King."

"It's his son, sir," Director Lucas started.

"His son?"

"He has a rare condition. Something I'd never heard of. Anyway, that is where the two payments to China come in."

"I don't understand. Why try to evade you about his son being sick?"

"Because the treatments for his son are illegal here, and he was trying to avoid getting caught up in something that could keep him from flying to China for the treatment. His son will die without it."

"And the investments in vaccine companies there?" the president said. "That not still suspicious to you?"

"We checked medical records here. His investment came after his son was diagnosed. He wanted to find a cure, and a subsequent vaccine to stop it from happening to someone else's son."

Gibbons was quiet for a moment. He thought about how he needed to relay this to King. King was still in danger if Warshaw had nothing to do with it. Because if it was Kuznetsov, the enemy could be coming for King and he was stranded in Barrow.

"You're sure? What did Warshaw have to say about meeting with Kuznetsov?"

"He said the meeting was short. Kuznetsov apparently had a grudge against Warshaw already," Director Lucas explained. "Something about funding being pulled in Russia at Kuznetsov's lab and moved to China because Warshaw had invested in China instead of Kuznetsov's lab. Warshaw said Kuznetsov was going on about how it ruined his chance to leave something special behind for his niece, who was an aspiring virologist as well. And guess who that was?"

"I don't have any idea. Who?"

"Veronika Kamenev."

"Why does that sound familiar?" the president said.

"Because she was the woman who was killed in the Moscow hangar when Sam interrupted their plans to pass off the samples."

The president's heart sank. King was completely unaware that he'd been with the enemy the entire time. Kuznetsov could be planning to kill him at any moment.

"I've got to go, Robert. I'll call you back!"

Gibbons ended the call and immediately dialed the number he had for King.

It rang once. Gibbons was pacing back and forth as long as the cord on the phone would let him.

The second ring came and went. What if he was too late?

"Pick up!" he shouted.

The third and fourth ring played out. Then it went to voice mail.

Why wasn't King answering his phone?

46

Barrow, Alaska, 3:05 p.m.

King and Cali got into her Jeep and drove out of the airport. King found both of Josiah's men at the airport and put them inside the plane with their rifles. King decided it was best to take the vials out of the briefcase and leave them on the plane. That way if something went wrong, he would at least not have to worry about the vials on top of his and Cali's survival. King rounded the bend just outside the airport, and his stomach dropped.

"Please tell me that's not—" King started to ask about the truck that had run off the side of the road, but he stopped when the answer was on the license plate. The sheriff's emblem on the left side of the plate confirmed what he was afraid of. His phone was vibrating in his pocket, but he was too focused on Josiah's truck and what the problem could be to answer it.

"Oh my God, that's Josiah's truck!" Cali said.

After getting off the phone with the president just a minute ago, he and Cali were driving to the jail to get Kuznetsov so King could take him back to Moscow. They'd hardly rounded the corner before he saw the truck. King slammed on the brakes and pulled to the side of the road. He and Cali jumped out and raced over to the truck. When King ran over to the driver's side door, he was shocked when he found no one inside.

King pulled his phone from his pocket. As he started to dial, he saw that the missed call was from DC. Probably the president confirming that Warshaw was in custody and they were going to work on wrapping things up. He opened his phone and scrolled to Josiah's number and pressed call.

Cali came around to his side. "Where the hell could they be?"

"I'm calling his phone now."

When they heard Josiah's phone ringing inside the truck, King knew something was dead wrong. Cali looked at him in horror. She opened the door and picked up his phone, then showed it to King.

"Shit!" King shouted and moved back toward Cali's Jeep.

"Something's wrong, X. He wouldn't have left his phone if they'd just broke down."

King didn't respond, and he climbed inside the Jeep. Cali realized his wheels were turning so she didn't continue to talk. He knew it in his bones at that moment that he'd made a monumental mistake in trusting Kuznetsov. Warshaw may very well still have a part in the whole thing, but Kuznetsov was just as guilty, if not more so. He didn't have time for self-loathing. He opened his phone and returned the president's call to the number that he'd missed.

"X?" the president answered.

"It's not just Warshaw, is it? It's Kuznetsov."

"Thank God you're okay. No, it's not Warshaw. Kuznetsov is behind it all. He set Warshaw up because of a grudge and so there would be a fall guy when the virus went national. Please tell me you have him!"

King's silence was answer enough.

"Damn it!" the president shouted. "If he gets away, he'll release the virus. Director Lucas just called me back. The CIA found a website on the dark web. They traced the musings of an account back to Kuznetsov's niece, Veronika—"

"Veronika? As in Sam's Veronika at the Moscow hangar?"

No wonder Kuznetsov had been so upset in the lab when he was given the news of her death. She was his niece.

"Yes, that Veronika," the president said. "But what I'm trying to tell you is that *she* is the one who recruited Vince Huang through this dark website. He was spewing hatred about the United States because he was fired, I guess. Well, she was doing the same, because apparently Kuznetsov's first wife was American, and she left him to go back to America. And Veronika's mother—Kuznetsov's sister—was killed in a car accident by an American tourist in Moscow. All of Veronika's posts were all about how they hate America and how it needs to be brought to its knees. X, Vince Huang and Veronika Kamenev were married last year."

King couldn't believe what he was hearing, but his mind had already shifted in two directions. One: where is

Kuznetsov, and what happened to Josiah? Two: Sam was in it even deeper than she knew, but at least she had already found Vince Huang.

"Sir," King said, "I have to find Kuznetsov. Send any military you can get out here from Fort Greely in Fairbanks. This will probably be over by then, but I don't want there to be any fallout here after it's over. They can help keep order. There are a lot of Russians here, and probably a lot more of them are here for reasons other than everyone thought."

"Okay. Don't let Kuznetsov leave Barrow, King. If he makes it out with those samples—"

"I have the samples, sir, but the ones lost in Moscow might already be en route. Shut everything down. Do not let anyone fly in from Russia. If it's not already too late. Any plane that does come in, whether commercial or private, better get a thorough search. It may mean the difference in a global pandemic."

"If someone is flying in private, there is no way we could police every airport," the president said.

"You'd better start now. Use the FBI, the CIA, the police departments, whatever you can to track all flight logs and to be ready. I have to go find Kuznetsov. Good luck."

"Good luck to you, son."

King ended the call and immediately dialed Dbie. She answered on the first ring.

"Hello?"

"Dbie, have you had a chance to comb through the bank account that Kuznetsov had emailed you about earlier?"

King knew Kuznetsov was the culprit, but he had to have help somewhere with funding. Even if it wasn't Warshaw, they needed to know who it was.

"X," Dbie said, "I never received an email from anyone about bank accounts."

If there was any doubt left in King's mind whether or not Kuznetsov was guilty, it had just been erased. And now that he thought about the phone call Kuznetsov made in front of him to the supposed banker, it was probably the very thing that set in motion everything that was happening now. Though he didn't speak any Russian on that call, whoever he called probably sounded all the alarms after Kuznetsov spoke only in English. That must have been the reason the guards played the game at the gate at Volkov Mining. King couldn't believe how convincing Kuznetsov had been. Then he recalled the moment in the underground lab when the guard had a clear shot at King but didn't take it because Kuznetsov was there. But they so easily shot the other two scientists only seconds later. If Kuznetsov wasn't the man, they wouldn't have cared to kill him either. Especially since it had been known that the vaccine was finished.

"X, you there? Everything all right?"

"No. It's not. But I have to go. Make sure you're available in case I need you. Start looking into who is the owner or the money behind Volkov Mining. There may be something there. I have to go find the bad guy, again."

"I'm on it. And this time it shouldn't be hard for you. I got a ping on my tracking software an hour or two ago. I'm assuming that was you since the tracker is in Barrow. Or did it just fall out of your holster?"

In the chaos, King hadn't had time to remember he'd slipped the tracker on the back of Kuznetsov's neck.

"Dbie, have I told you lately that I love you?"

"It's been a while."

King ended the call and pulled up the tracking app.

"Now what?" Cali said. "You don't think he'll hurt Josiah, do you? What if we can't find him?"

"Oh, we're gonna find him. I just hope it isn't too late."

47

Moscow, Russia, 2:05 a.m.

Patrick punched Vince Huang in the stomach for the third time, and again he doubled over in pain.

"Where is she?" Sam shouted. "I know you know. Tell me or I will shoot you right now!"

Vince's grunt of pain slowly tuned into a laugh. "You can kill me if you want. But you're too late."

Sam looked at Patrick. "You know the rumor around Langley is that you have a hell of a temper. I saw a little bit of that when you saved my ass back at the deli. I'm going to need a bit more of it now. What do you say?"

Vince raised up wearing a bloody smile. "Are you two for real? Are you seriously trying 'good cop, bad cop' on me?"

Patrick reached forward, grabbed hold of Vince's right hand by his fingers. With a violent amount of torque, he bent all four of them in the wrong direction. The cracking of his bones echoed beneath that bridge. He screamed in pain.

"Not sure there are any good cops here, Vince," Patrick told him. "Your other hand is next. Tell us where they're hiding the woman and I'll spare you a limb."

Every man has his breaking point, and Vince Huang's was broken fingers. Sam wasn't impressed. She'd seen men half his size hold out longer.

"She's close! Shit! Please stop!" Vince doubled over, clutching at his hand. "I'll take you to her."

Patrick opened the back door of the car and shoved him inside. He and Sam got in the front.

Sam turned around and put her gun on him. "Where?"

"Just keep driving this direction. It's only a few blocks."

Patrick pulled forward.

"Who was the Russian man that called me from her phone?" Sam said.

"What? I don't know. What Russian man?"

"Don't play dumb. We can pull the car over again. I know it wasn't either of those two back at the apartment, so who was he?"

Vince put both hands up, his four fingers still bent the wrong way. "I don't know, I swear!"

Sam swung the barrel of the gun, striking him in the crooked fingers. After a shout of pain he yelled, "Okay!" He regained his composure. "Turn right up here. The man is my wife's brother, okay? Real mean son of a bitch, too, so you'd better hope you don't run into him."

"*Am I* going to run into him when we get here?" Sam said.

"It's the brick building on the left. She's in the basement."

Patrick swerved off the road and pulled into a parking space.

"You didn't answer my question," Sam said.

"What?"

"Are we going to run into . . . what's his name?"

"I-I—"

Sam reached back and shoved the gun against his forehead. "Never mind. We'll find out his name."

"Wait!" Vince squinted his eyes as he shouted. "Wait. It's Artem. Artem Kamenev. And I hope you do find him in there. You'll get what you deserve!"

Patrick got out of the car, opened the back door, pulled Vince over as he begged for his life, and hit him so hard in the forehead that the lights instantly went out.

"I had it handled," Sam said as she got out of the car.

"I know. I was just tired of his mouth. And people are easier to tie up when they're unconscious."

Sam shrugged. She couldn't argue with his logic. His blunt-force mentality reminded her a lot of X. Patrick went to the trunk and came back with a rope. While Patrick tied him up, she took in the building. There were no other cars in the parking lot. The one street lamp on the corner wasn't much help with lighting. From the looks of it, they were at the back of the building. Patrick shut the door and locked the car before he walked up beside her.

Sam pulled out her phone and sent Dbie a text: *Find out who Artem Kamenev is.*

She put her phone back in her pocket. "It's awfully quiet."

"Too quiet," Patrick agreed. "How's your arm?"

"Wasn't bothering me until you just mentioned it. Thanks."

The two of them gave a laugh but not a hearty one. They both knew the trouble that was staring them in the face. Sam was about to make a move when her phone vibrated. She pulled it from her pocket—Dbie had already responded. Sam almost didn't look because she figured that to have texted back so quickly, it was probably Dbie's standard *I'm on it.* But it wasn't.

Dbie's text read, *Already know who Artem is. X had me digging on Kuznetsov and his name came up. He's Kuznetsov's nephew. Lots of reports tying him to the Russian mob. When I dug deeper, he's the principle owner of Volkov Mining in Barrow. This entire thing was set up by Kuznetsov and his family. Need anything else?*

Sam was dumbfounded. She texted back: *Not right now. Thx.*

"Artem is Russian mob," Sam said. "Know anyone else in the city who can help?"

"Not even one." Patrick pulled his gun as he answered.

"You don't have to go in here," Sam told him. "This isn't your fight."

"This is all of our fight. It's what we signed up for."

Sam was happy he felt that way. She was good on her own, but having to try to save Zhanna while staying alive was harder than just shooting up a place. And she could tell by Patrick's performance so far that he'd do whatever it took.

Sam took the first step toward the door when suddenly the door to the building burst outward. She came within a hair of shooting Zhanna right in the chest. If it hadn't been for her fiery red hair catching the light of the street lamp, she would have killed her. Sam shot her hand over to Patrick and knocked his arms to the side just in case, shouting out of instinct,

"Don't shoot! She's one of us!"

48

SAM WAS ABLE TO MOVE PATRICK'S ARM AND KEEP HIM FROM shooting when Zhanna came running out of the building. At first Zhanna ducked and pulled herself into a squatted fetal position. When she noticed the gun was Sam's, and heard her shout, "She's one of ours," Zhanna stood and ran over to Sam, throwing her arms around her.

"Are you all right?" Sam said. As she squeezed Zhanna with one arm, she kept her gun hand trained on the door.

"Yes."

When Zhanna pulled away, she could see that she had been slapped around a bit, but overall she was incredibly lucky.

"Is there anyone inside?" Sam was still worried about all of their safety.

"No, they just left."

"Why would they leave you here unguarded?" Patrick said.

"Who are you?" Zhanna said.

Sam answered for him. "He's CIA. Already saved my ass. Do we need to be on the move?"

"Yes. Right now. I'm so glad you are here. They are taking the virus to America!"

"Right now?" Sam said.

"We must go to airport, now!"

"Wait," Patrick said. "Why would they say this in front of you? They wouldn't want you to know."

"Because they didn't know I spoke English, so they used it around me. That, and I'm supposed to be dead. A man was supposed to be here already to kill me. I heard the name Vince."

Sam shot a look at Patrick. Sam had saved Zhanna's life by coming to the meeting place early that night. But she didn't have time to be thankful.

"Patrick, can you put him in the trunk? We have to go!"

"What?" Zhanna said.

"Vince. We found him before he found you."

Zhanna was at a loss for words.

"They didn't happen to say which airport, did they?" Sam said.

"No, but driver said twenty-five miles. That is Sheremetyevo."

"You know how to get there?"

"Yes, I'll drive!"

Sam and Zhanna jumped in the front of the car, and after Patrick closed Vince in the trunk, he hopped in the back. Zhanna hit the road and swerved her way toward the airport. This was the first chance Sam had to ask Zhanna why she was with Kuznetsov's assistant, Veronika, at the hangar earlier. Sam had thought about it a couple of times and couldn't come up with a good reason. But she had to do one more thing before she asked her about it.

Sam pulled her phone and dialed Director Lucas.

"Give me some good news, Sam," Lucas answered.

"I need you to do whatever you can to stop any planes from leaving the Sheremetyevo Airport. Commercial or private."

"In Moscow? Sam, there's no way I can do that."

"Then prepare to lose millions of lives in America."

Sam was never melodramatic, but she didn't have time to beat around the bush. This was as serious of a request as she had ever made.

"You're sure?" Lucas said.

"The virus is on its way to Sheremetyevo now. The '*wait and see*' approach will burn us this time. I'm sure of it."

"Let me call the president. Are you there at the airport?"

"We're on our way, and we know who we're looking for. Artem Kamenev."

At the same time Sam said the man's name, Zhanna shot her a look, and Director Lucas nearly shouted, "Kamenev?"

"Yes, why?" Sam said.

Sam could tell by the look on Zhanna's face that she already knew what Director Lucas was about to tell her.

"As in Veronika Kamenev?"

Sam covered the phone and spoke to Zhanna. "Is Artem related to Veronika?"

"Her brother," Zhanna confirmed.

In an instant the entire operation came together for Sam.

She uncovered the phone and spoke to Lucas. "Yes, her

brother. He is the majority owner of Volkov Mining. Well, his holding company is."

"Wow. It was right under our nose the entire time. When we researched Volkov, his name did not come up. How did you know that?"

"Dbie Johnson uncovered it," Sam answered. "I'll have her call you. But please stop the planes or have Artem arrested on site. Whatever you have to do!"

"I'll call you back when I know something." Director Lucas ended the call.

"The man who captured me is Veronika's brother?" Zhanna questioned immediately.

"Yes," Sam said. "And get this, Artem and Veronika are Dmitry Kuznetsov's nephew and niece. They've used mafia money and virology education to construct the super virus."

"Unbelievable," Zhanna said. "We had no idea Dmitry Kuznetsov was involved. We thought he was dead after disappearing a while back."

Zhanna saying "we" triggered what Sam was about to ask Zhanna before Director Lucas called. About how Zhanna became caught up in all of this in the first place.

"Who's we?" Sam said. "How did you get involved in all of this?"

"We means FIS. Russian Intelligence. I was coming off a private job and had no work. I was going to call you, but before I could, FIS said they needed me. They overpaid me to be 'security' for Veronika. This was my first day."

"You can't be serious," Patrick chimed in from the back.

"I no shit you," Zhanna said. "First day. I was barely briefed on what Russian government was concerned about with Veronika before my lunch with her this morning. It was about mob ties. I was told to get close to her.

We had a good lunch, and now she's dead. But I learned a lot."

"I guess so," Sam said. "Not to blow your mind again, but her husband was the man coming to kill you."

"You are shitting me?" Zhanna nearly swerved off the road as she drove onto the freeway.

"I'm not."

Then Sam thought of something she wished she'd thought of earlier. "How does Artem know he has the virus in those vials he took from you?"

Zhanna glanced over with a puzzled look on her face. "I-I don't know."

"Because the vials I trashed to keep from getting shot outside the hangar could have been either the virus *or* the vaccine."

Patrick leaned forward between them. "You mean this Artem guy on the way to the airport might not even know he could only be carrying the vaccine?"

"They were not marked," Sam said. "I handed Zhanna the two on the left side, and I took the ones on the right. There is no way Artem could know what he has."

"Then Artem may not be dangerous at all," Zhanna said. "But how can we know? It is difference between no problem at all and catastrophe."

Zhanna was right. How could they know? If they could find out which samples Sam trashed and which ones Artem Kamenev had, it would mean everything. There was no way Sam could find out. Not from what they had with them.

"Stop the car!" Sam shouted.

Zhanna laid on the brakes, and the car skidded to a stop on the side of the road. Sam jumped out of the car and ran around to the trunk.

"What are you doing?" Patrick jumped out with her.

"Maybe he knows," Sam said. "Vince knew about the incident at the hangar. He's been involved this entire time. Maybe he knows the order Kuznetsov placed the samples in!"

Patrick popped the trunk and yanked Vince out. Sam shut the trunk, and Patrick slammed Vince against it.

Sam got in Vince's face. "What order are the vials placed in the briefcase?"

"What? I don't know what you're talking about!"

Sam pulled out her gun and shot him right in the thigh. Through his screams of pain, she shouted at him. "Tell me or the next bullet is in your neck!"

Vince shouted in pain again. Sam raised her gun.

"Okay! I don't know. He changes it every time in case something like today ever happened. You shot my leg!"

"Bullshit!" Sam pressed the gun against his neck. "Tell me the order!"

"I would know if I was the one with the samples, but I didn't bring these! I swear!" Vince pleaded.

"So you didn't watch your wife die today?"

Genuine emotion moved over his face. "If I had been there, she wouldn't be dead! This wasn't my run. I was already here for all of my testing after Atqasuk. That was my last run. Just don't shoot me!"

"You let the virus go in Atqasuk and the other towns in Alaska, didn't you?" Sam said.

Sam felt the swell of anger rising. The man in front of her had been responsible for more than two hundred deaths already. Maybe more in Atqasuk, the latest Alaskan town to fall ill.

"Last chance," Sam said as she pressed the gun deeper

into his neck. "Tell me the order, or you die where you stand."

"I-I don't know the order—"

Blood splattered onto Sam before the sound of the gunshot registered or before she realized Patrick had moved his gun underneath Vince's chin.

"We have to go," Patrick said. "He didn't know the order of the vials. We need to get to the airport and stop Artem."

Vince's body folded over and thudded against the pavement. Sam put away her gun, then wiped the blood from her face with the bottom of her thermal shirt. The three of them moved back toward the car without saying a word. Sam was happy she didn't have to pull the trigger, but she would have liked at least a heads-up.

Zhanna pulled back onto the road and sped off toward the airport. That was when it occurred to Sam that she had one last chance at figuring out the order of the vials, as well as whether Artem Kamenev was heading toward America with samples that could destroy the United States or with harmless tubes of a vaccine that wouldn't infect a single person.

Her best friend and partner in crime was with the actual source of both at that very moment, Dmitry Kuznetsov. Sam pulled out her phone and made the most important call of her life.

She called Alexander King.

49

ALEXANDER KING WAS FOLLOWING the tracking app on his phone from the passenger seat. He and Cali had switched seats so he could concentrate on managing phone calls and running Kuznetsov down. They were getting close to Kuznetsov's location when King's phone rang. It was a private number. King put the phone on speaker so he could still see the tracker, and answered the call without speaking.

"Bring the samples to me and I will give you back your friend."

Cali shot a hopeful look in King's direction.

"He's not my friend."

Cali frowned and went back to the road.

"Then he will die," Kuznetsov said.

King could see Cali's grip on the steering wheel tighten. He wished she didn't have to hear this, but he didn't have a choice.

"Then he dies. You think I would trade the tens of thousands of American lives, maybe more, for the life of one man I barely know? You must not know how things work in our country. Sacrifices must be made."

"Have it your way."

The call ended.

"X, I know this is none of my business, and I know that tough decisions are going to have to be made, but can you really just let them kill Josiah?"

King was quiet. Cali fought her emotions as she nodded her head. He didn't have time to deal with what she cared about, no matter how much he cared about her.

"I get it," she said. "This is more than I can understand and I won't say another word."

King checked the tracking app again. "It looks like we aren't far."

"How close?" Cali said.

"Half a mile, maybe."

"He's at the police station. It's the only thing that close on this road."

"You're sure?" he asked.

"Positive. And I know a back way in. The night Josiah came on to me, we snuck in the back. He was trying to show off, but I didn't like him like that."

"Can you take us there without them seeing us?"

Cali jerked the Jeep off the road and onto some rough terrain. "I think so."

"Perfect." King contemplated not saying anything more, but he just couldn't help it. "I don't think they'll kill him. That's why I said what I said. The vials are too important to Kuznetsov."

"You don't have to explain." They bumped over some

more road, and then she killed the headlights. "You can put the tracker away, that's the station."

King squinted into the dying twilight. What she was referring to was no more than what looked like a couple of elongated shacks glued together, backed up to a wooded area. It looked like there were a couple of SUVs out front as well as what he swore was one of the military trucks from the gate at Volkov. Then they passed into a row of trees themselves.

"We should walk from here," Cali said as she slowed the Jeep.

"There is no *we*, Cali," King said. "You have to go back to the plane and be ready to go. Josiah's men can keep you and the samples safe."

King grabbed the briefcase from the floorboard behind him.

"Then why are you taking the empty briefcase?" she asked.

"Kuznetsov doesn't know it's empty."

"I don't understand," Cali said. "Why don't you just leave? You have what you came for. You have the virus and the vaccine. Why risk your life if Josiah's doesn't matter?"

"I never said Josiah's life . . . Look, I don't have what I came for. If I let Kuznetsov leave here, I will never find him again. And just because I managed the vials doesn't mean he won't try this again somewhere else."

Cali nodded. "Just be careful." She began to lean toward him when his phone rang. It was Sam.

"Sam, you all right?"

"No. X, I need to talk to Kuznetsov right now."

"That's not possible."

"He's not with you?"

"No, but I'm about to get him back."

"Damn it!" Sam shouted.

"What's wrong? How could he possibly help you?"

"Because the virus could be on the move right now. To the airport. I just don't know if the Artem has vials of virus or vaccine. Kuznetsov would have been the last one to be able to tell us the order."

"Sam, you have to stop Artem from getting on a plane. You know he'll be headed for the US."

"You don't think I know that?" Sam shouted. "If he's flying private, we'll never make it. And we'll never know where he actually ends up flying to. He won't go straight to the US. If he's smart, he'll go somewhere else and try to drive it across the border."

King's skin began to crawl. All the progress he'd made there in Barrow was going to be for nothing if the virus got out from Moscow. There had to be a way to stop him.

"You told Lucas to shut down travel?" King said.

"Of course, but by the time it goes through the channels, even if the president himself is making the calls, it will be too late. You know that."

King shifted in his seat toward the window to see if there was any movement at the police station, but he couldn't see through the trees. He needed to go before Kuznetsov either moved again or more of his men came to his aid. When he shifted back toward Cali, ready to end the call, he felt something bulge in his pocket.

Kuznetsov's notebook.

"Wait, Sam, I might have something."

King shot his hand in his pocket and pulled out the notebook.

"I don't know what will be in it," King told Sam. "But I have Kuznetsov's lab notebook."

"Oh, please, God, be the answer," Sam said. "Vince Huang said Kuznetsov always changed the order of the vials. He said he changed the order of them every time so no one would know but him. Please tell me he wrote it down!"

King handed the phone to Cali. "Hold the light on the notebook, please." King began thumbing through it. The first few pages were nothing but notes about the lab equipment. Not a good start.

What Sam said finally registered. "Wait, you have Huang. Just ask him the order!"

"*Had him, you mean*," Sam said. "He's recently deceased. He didn't know the order because he wasn't the one who brought the samples to the hangar in Moscow."

"Shit, okay. Does that mean you have Zhanna?"

King stopped thumbing to take in Sam's answer.

"We do. She's fine. Now please worry about the notebook!"

It was a sigh of relief to know that Zhanna was okay. The deeper he went into the notebook, King saw more of the same meaningless notes. Then he noticed that every page was dated at the top. Kuznetsov telling him that he documented *everything* kept running through his mind. He skipped a chunk of pages to find the date he thought correlated with the first time the town in Alaska began getting sick. There was nothing on the first couple of pages.

"X, we are running out of time!" Sam urged.

"That's it!" King shouted. He couldn't believe what he'd found. As he ran his finger down the sheet, the name of the first town to get sick was there, with four groups of two letters beside it: Vi Va Vi Va.

"Vi Va Vi Va," King read them aloud. "That's what he wrote next to the first town's name! Let me check the second one."

"Virus Vaccine Virus Vaccine?" Sam said.

"That has to be it!" Cali said.

"I think so too, but hold on," King said.

"Please, God, let it be Vi Vi Va Va when you get to the Moscow samples!"

King found the right dates for the next town. "Va Vi Va Vi for the second one. Let me skip to the last few days."

He jumped ahead to a few days ago. There were notes about the vaccine working, just as Kuznetsov had said. And disgusting notes about what was going on in Atqasuk, the last town that was getting sick. Then he finally found the word *Moscow*. Beside it was the order of the vials that had traveled there and that Sam had intercepted at the hangar. He couldn't believe it.

"Va Va Vi Vi!"

"What? Say that again!" Sam shouted.

"Va Va Vi Vi! That's what you wanted right?"

"Artem Kamenev only has the vaccine!" Sam shouted. There was cheering in the background of her phone call. "I trashed the ones on the right. I destroyed the virus! He can't hurt anyone!"

It was absolutely incredible news. He doubted in the history of mankind that one line in a notebook ever saved so many lives. It was a stroke of luck, but those are the kinds of things you need in the end when dealing with these types of situations. Like everything else in life, you can do everything right and still lose. This time, they were lucky. King could now focus all of his energy on making the man pay for all the lives he'd destroyed, and even the ones he had been about to ruin.

"Sam, I have to go. Make sure you don't let that man get away. Even if he does only have the vaccine."

"I'll do my best. And X?"

"Yeah?"

"Say hello to Kuznetsov for me," Sam said, "in the way only you know how to say it."

"Don't worry, Sam. I'll send your warmest regards."

50

Cali explained to King what he would find once he opened the back door of the police station. There was a mud room of sorts just inside, then a secure door that you could only get through by being buzzed in, unless you had a key. She said they buzzed people in by checking you on camera and then letting you in. Josiah had explained this to her the night he took her there. She said if King could make it through that door, there was a short hallway with offices on both sides, then a door that led to rows of cells, then another secure door that led to the lobby of the jailhouse.

King happily accepted a brief kiss from Cali, but as soon as he opened the door to get out of the Jeep, he forgot she ever existed, at least for the time being. He stepped out into the subzero air, but he didn't feel it. He decided to leave the empty briefcase in the Jeep. There would be no time for cloak-and-dagger once he made it inside. Cali pulled away in the Jeep behind him to go back to the airplane, but he didn't hear it. The only thing he took in was the path through the trees that led to one of the most despicable human beings on the planet.

King knew he was walking into a situation where he was completely outnumbered. And entirely outgunned. But he knew it wouldn't matter. He'd seen the extent of training these men had. Short of a lucky shot, they had no chance. It was the equivalent of putting someone in a boxing ring with the heavyweight champion of the world, when all they'd ever experienced were bar fights. Sure, in one out of a million matches, a bar fighter might land that one magical punch. But the odds were better of hitting the lottery.

To perform these type of missions, you had to have that mentality. That confidence. Some would call it arrogance, but as King himself would explain it, it's simply the facts. Considering the thousands of hours of training it took to be the type of killer King was, it didn't leave people room for luck. Not people like these Russian guards whose combat skills were limited to maybe having joined a police force at some point in their lives. King was about to chew through them.

King walked to the edge of the trees. He was only about fifty feet from the back of the police station. The first gift from the gods of war was a guard sitting outside the back door. It was his ticket through the secure door inside. When Cali was telling him about the station, he'd expected there would be someone watching the back door, so this didn't come as a surprise.

King had on him the AR-15 formerly strapped onto the upper body of a Volkov guard. He also had his Glock in the concealed holster at his back, and his silent killer, the Chris Reeve Sebenza knife in his pocket. In front of him a yellow light hung over the door. Below it, in what looked like fourteen layers of clothing, sat his first victim. There were no security cameras. They must have saved them all for the first room inside the door.

King reached down and picked up a thick piece of a fallen tree branch. Snow was trickling down from the sky, and the quiet was almost deafening. There was a dumpster about ten feet to the guard's left. King threw the stick as hard as he could. His throw was a little short, but it bounced up and dinged the metal dumpster pretty hard. The guard jumped up, aimed his gun toward the dumpster, and moved in that direction as he shouted something in Russian.

King thumbed open the blade on his knife and moved from the trees. He stalked his prey, running up behind the guard before he ever knew someone was there. He jabbed the blade in the man's neck three times. The first step in stopping the madman inside was done. When the guard fell to the ground, King removed his ushanka. King knew the warm hat by name because Zhanna had told him about it during a crew's night out a couple of years ago. King put the ushanka on his head and pulled the ear covers down. He then removed the magazine from the guard's AR-15 and shoved it in his coat pocket. The last thing he took was a set of keys out of the guard's pocket.

He pulled the ushanka down as far as he could on his head without impairing his vision as he tried the first key on the door. Nothing. He tried the second key, then the third, but none of them worked. Which made sense, because this man wasn't an employee of the Barrow Police Department. He was just another Russian thug. That's when gift number two came to him. The door handle moved down on its own, and the door eased open. When he heard a man inside say something in Russian, King took a step back. He couldn't kill him inside—it would get caught on camera—he needed the man to move outside.

The man said more words in Russian coupled with what sounded like someone's name. King figured the guard outside was supposed to knock when he wanted in, and the guard inside would open the door for him. The man who opened the door finally stepped out. King grabbed him by the rifle strap that was looped around his chest and yanked him outside. He dropped his knife in the doorjamb so it wouldn't close behind him. The guard rose to his feet but was distracted by the bloody mess his comrade had just made over by the dumpster.

King stepped forward and Thai kicked the man in the knee. His leg crumpled and he moaned in pain. King followed that with a knee to his chin and his head whipped back unconscious. King was never happy about killing people who were just doing their job, but he couldn't let them keep him from doing his. He crouched down beside the man and wrenched his neck in a way that he would never come back to life. A sound like breaking a neck is one a man never gets used to. But it was necessary.

He turned and walked over to the door. He pulled his knife from the doorjamb, hung his head down low, and walked inside. The white florescent lights above him were bright—a stark contrast to the darkness he was about to bring to every man inside.

51

KING DIDN'T LOOK UP AT THE CAMERAS IN THE HOLDING ROOM inside the police station. He just stared forward at the secured door. He knew they could see him.

A man's voice speaking Russian came over the speaker. In King's mind, the man had asked if he was ready for a shift change already. So he nodded his head and gave a thumbs-up. It was all he had.

When the door buzzed, King slid his hand to the small of his back. He still had the AR-15 strapped around his torso, but he knew he could be more accurate inside with the Glock.

As the buzz sound continued, he closed his eyes and tried to picture what awaited him on the other side. Cali had said it was a hallway of offices, before another secured door. No one in the entire station mattered to King except Kuznetsov. It didn't matter if there were ten men in front of him when he opened the door; he had to find Kuznetsov and eliminate him first—even if someone else had the drop on him and it cost him his life. Kuznetsov could not live to do this again.

Before King grabbed the door handle, he removed the glove on his shooting hand. He was going to have to be at his absolute best, and the glove would only slow his feel for the trigger. He reached for the door handle, pulled down, then pulled the door toward him. He raised his gun as he stepped through. As it did every time he was in these life-and-death situations, everything began to move in slow motion.

The man walking toward him was in military fatigues. His eyes widened when he noticed King bringing up a gun, but it was too late. King shot once, and the bullet hit somewhere around the left eye. Through a pink mist, King searched for Kuznetsov's wild white hair and wide nose. Instead, his eyes found two more men, both of them reaching for their guns. It was too late for the man on the left; King squeezed twice and both landed somewhere in the chest. King calculated in a millisecond that there was a chance the other man could get his shot off first, so he dove through the doorway of the office beside him. He heard four loud bangs as he crouched down low. Then he leaned out into the hallway and shot the man, sending bullets into his leg, then somewhere around his neck. The next man appeared about five feet behind the guard he'd just shot. King had heard the door buzz through the gunfire. He shot twice, but both his bullets hit the wall just beyond the man's head. The guard's gun was up and returning fire. King fell back into the office onto his back.

The guard stopped firing and shouted in Russian. More men were coming. King rolled over, staying as low as he could until his head and arms were outside the doorway. He shot two times, and before the man could jump inside the office on his right, King had hit him. The door leading into the cell portion of the jailhouse shut. King wasn't overly worried that they would try to usher Kuznetsov out the front door into one of the SUVs. King still had the tracking chip on Kuznetsov, but he didn't want to take this show on the road. He wanted to end it right now. Instead of walking down the hall, he moved back inside the office and lifted the only window in the small room.

The door buzzed again out in the hallway—an alarm of sorts letting King know someone else was coming. He put one leg out the window, then the other, and dropped down to the ground below. As soon as his feet landed, he sprinted for the front of the police station. He slid his Glock back inside his holster as he ran, then spun the AR-15 so he was holding it in his hands. When he got to the edge of the front corner of the station, he stopped. He peeked around the corner and watched as two men came running out the front. He had no idea what was going on inside the jailhouse, but he was sure someone had told them to go secure the perimeter before bringing Kuznetsov out.

King let the AR-15 hang from his shoulder by the strap as he shot his hand in his pocket. The guard was running fast for the corner, but he managed to pull the knife and open the blade. King put his back against the wall and bent his knees to steady himself. He pulled his arm up about chin high, and as soon as the man rounded the corner, King leaned in with an elbow to the jaw that knocked the man completely off his feet. Almost as soon as the guard's back hit the ground, King slammed the knife into his neck so he couldn't scream. He closed the blade of his knife and placed it in his pocket. Then he pulled his Glock once again. He had five shots left.

He took another look around the corner. This time he noticed a camera in the eave of the roof, right beside the floodlight. It was decision time. If he sat back and waited, he was sure Kuznetsov would eventually come out. This would make Kuznetsov an easy target. The problem with waiting was that someone could easily come up King's back side and end the good run he was on.

The risk wasn't worth the consequences. He'd rather move on his own terms. And that's exactly what he did.

52

KING GLANCED OVER HIS SHOULDER ONE LAST TIME. HE WAS glad he did. Through a squint King could see someone's head poking out of the window he'd jumped from earlier. He decided it was best to have a larger magazine to shoot with going into the unknown, so he swapped the Glock for the AR-15. It was time to move.

He surged around the corner and right up to the glass door that led to the end of his mission. His gun was ready, so he was able to shoot the guard standing in front of the door with two squeezes. He continued to fire even though the man had dropped to the ground. He was laying cover for himself. Not ideal, but it was all he had.

With his bullets slamming into the walls inside, and the chaos of the glass door shattering, King moved immediately to his left so he was in front of the window. The curtain was pulled back, and he saw exactly what he was hoping to see: Dmitry Kuznetsov's face. His face was glaring worriedly through the square window on the other side of the secured door that led further inside the jailhouse. King raised his gun, but before he could shoot, he saw something move out of the corner of his left eye. He instantly dropped to the ground, and bullets crashed through the window where his head had just been. He Army-crawled forward with his elbows, his gun still fixed in his hands. Through the busted front door, King could see a man was crouched behind a desk. When the guard raised up, King shot him dead.

King popped up to his feet and jumped sideways to put his back against the wall. Again it crossed his mind that these men had no business guarding anyone. In this situation, Kuznetsov's loss was King's gain. He showed the barrel of his gun through the front door. As the bullets came, he spun back to his right and aimed through the window. The man was a sitting duck, shooting where King was and not where he was going to be. King took three shots: two hit him, and he was down. He scanned the rest of the lobby, and no one else was there. King was in perfect position. Kuznetsov would have to come through him to get to a vehicle. Before King went inside, though, his mind did a perimeter check. One of the two guards who had come through the front door a moment ago and gone around the opposite side of the station had yet to return. And at least one more man was sticking his head out the window. King needed to locate them before he moved inside. The second he walked through that front door, his back would be exposed. So he bypassed it and went back to the side of the station he'd just come from.

King didn't take time to have a look first; he didn't want to give anyone a chance to see him. This was where the AR-15 came in handy. He walked right around the corner, already firing before he saw the man running toward him. With a small correction in aim, he sprayed the man in the torso. When he dropped dead, a man at the far end of the station came into view. Before King could shoot, the guard ducked back behind the dumpster. King made a mental note not to forget about that man.

He backpedaled to the front again. No one had come running. King figured by that point he must have devastatingly thinned the herd. He ditched the AR once again for his Glock as he opened the shattered front door. There were three dead men inside and a woman he assumed was Elaine. Josiah had said her name, days ago it seemed, when she patched the president's call to him in King's living room.

Kuznetsov's face was no longer in the door's small square window. King walked up to it and found a small hallway like the one he'd been in earlier. The only stretch of the jailhouse he hadn't seen now were the cells. They were right in the middle, according to Cali. And since the hall was empty, he figured that was where Kuznetsov had moved to.

King opened the door and quickly checked the offices. All four of them were empty. There was one more door separating him and the cells. It didn't have a window, so he would have to go in blind. The only other thing that he hoped to see when he opened the door, besides Kuznetsov cowering in a corner, was Josiah. If he wasn't in one of the cells, more than likely he was dead.

King was worried about the other guard he'd seen at the back of the jailhouse. He would've had time to come in through the back door. It was likely he wouldn't be able to get through the doors because no one was manning the buzzers, but King couldn't be too careful. He ducked inside one of the offices and grabbed a rolling chair. He opened the door without moving in front of it. No one made a sound at first. Then he heard Josiah shout.

"He's got a gun!"

King shoved the rolling chair around the door and through the doorway. Gunshots echoed through the enclosed space. They were almost deafening, but they weren't aimed at the door; the bullets instead were hitting the chair King had tossed inside. King's sense of slow motion returned. He stepped around the door and saw Josiah standing in front and to the right of Kuznetsov. Kuznetsov was firing the gun from behind Josiah with his left hand. That's when Josiah made the move that saved his own life, diving to the ground and leaving Kuznetsov exposed. By the time Kuznetsov's eyes found King's, King had already shot him twice in the chest.

Kuznetsov slid down the wall onto his ass. He dropped his gun and clutched his chest. King couldn't savor the moment, however, because he heard the door to the lobby open behind him. He turned and shot the three remaining rounds in his magazine. The poor guard never even saw it coming.

"Holy shit, you did it," Josiah said. "You fucking maniac. You did it!"

King ignored Josiah's shouts, holstered his gun, and walked over to Kuznetsov. King hadn't made it in time to see his evil actually leave the earth—Kuznetsov was already dead. His long stare into nothing would forever be burned into King's memory. King had killed a lot of people in his time as a soldier and special operator, but none was more satisfying than this one. Kuznetsov had already single-handedly killed a couple hundred people. But it was the possible millions of lives saved that made it so fulfilling for King.

King stood over the dead monster of a man and took a long, deep breath. It was finally over. With the vials of the virus and the vaccine safe in his possession, and the only man on earth who could recreate it lying dead in front of him, King's work in that frozen hellhole was done.

And he couldn't have been happier about that.

EPILOGUE

Four Days Later
  The Cayman Islands

Another warm breeze blew across the pool area at the boutique resort in the Cayman Islands. The palm trees swayed, the ocean waves crashed, and Alexander King hadn't been as happy as he was in that moment, in years. Over by the tiki hut, a steel drum band waxed melodically, the singer saying something about tropical drinks melting in your hand. King set down his book and watched Sam as she laughed with Cali at the swim-up bar in the pool. He almost felt whole. The only thing that was missing was his closest friend, Kyle Hamilton.

King wasn't sure he would ever have a moment like this again. The day he decided to disappear, he'd made the decision to sacrifice these sorts of pleasures. However, after watching Dmitry Kuznetsov stare into the afterlife, he realized that the entire point of fighting the bad guys was so that he, and everyone else in the free world, could have the opportunity to drink too much by the pool by day and make love to someone extraordinarily beautiful by night. And that was exactly how King had spent the last two days. And after the dark, frozen, and murderous two weeks he'd just spent in Barrow, Alaska, it was an absolute breath of sun-warmed fresh air.

By the time King and Sam filled out all their paperwork and went through the debriefing process, Nigel Warshaw had been cleared of all wrongdoing. Kuznetsov had really tried to stick it to him—all the way down to the plane they'd used that had been linked to the holding company of one of Warshaw's former colleagues. Turned out, Kuznetsov had his own plane, which was funded by his nephew Artem's mob money, painted the same color and gave it the same tail number, all in an attempt to throw people off the scent. It had almost worked.

Director Lucas had been cleared as well. He found it funny that Kuznetsov had included him in his little charade. President Gibbons did not. President Gibbons wasn't finding a lot of things funny now since he'd been elected. Half the media in existence managed to blame him for risking the lives of every single American. Saying that he played with their lives by not giving the American people more information. They'd been spinning lies for more than seventy-two hours. King was actually there when all of it was going down, and he didn't know any of the stories they were telling.

Because they didn't happen.

This is what happens when you give biased people the freedom to print or report whatever the hell they want. King just shrugged all of that off. He'd learned a long time ago not to let what the media—*any* of the media, right or left—has to say bother him, no matter what his political or social beliefs. Because all they wanted, whether from one extreme or the other, was for you to believe what they believed. And they would say anything to make that happen.

Cali motioned for King to join them in the pool. He'd heard someone say one time that most of the world's problems could be solved by a swim-up margarita bar. At the moment, he couldn't think of one argument against that. He stepped down into the cool water, the sun high in the sky baking his broad shoulders. He waded over to Sam and Cali, and Cali wrapped her arms around him.

"Hey, good lookin'," she said. Her smile dialed up to a ten. Then she kissed him. Her breath was a mix of sweet limes and some coconut lip balm. Her skin was hot, and her body was the best scenery on the entire island.

"Disgusting," Sam said. She couldn't help herself. But King knew by the way she had buddied up to Cali that she liked her. That was a first for Sam, who still had a patch over her left shoulder. She said the wound was healing nicely. Patrick O'Connor had done a good job not doing any permanent damage.

Cali pulled away, reached for the bar, and handed Sam and King a shot each. The three of them tapped the plastic of their cups and threw their drinks back. The warm tequila burned all the way to King's stomach.

"Hey, Sam, guess you've taken two shots this week now." King nodded to her shoulder as he grinned from ear to ear. Shocker, Sam didn't find it amusing.

"Was that a dad joke?" Cali laughed.

King shrugged.

The bartender walked over and handed King a large cup

of golden juice, a little umbrella sticking out of the ice. "Your margarita, Mister Bond," he said.

King winked at Sam. "That's James Bond."

"Yes, sir," the bartender said, half smiling. "You've mentioned that a couple of times."

Sam almost refused to get his credentials made when he insisted that James Bond was the name he wanted to go by for the weekend. Finally, she'd given in. Kyle would have thought it was hilarious. Just like Cali had, because it was her idea. She was still laughing when King took his first sip. It was delicious.

"That never gets old," Cali said about King's cover name.

"You sure about that?" Sam smiled. The ice queen was melting.

It was turning into one of life's better days. Then, from the bar beside Sam, her phone began to ring.

"Don't answer that," King told her.

Sam lifted the phone to check the number. "It's Director Lucas."

"Then *definitely* don't answer that."

Sam set down her drink and picked up the phone. Cali took the opportunity to snuggle in close to King. Her sun-kissed face glowed, and her dirty-blonde hair blew in the breeze.

"You did say this vacation wouldn't last long," Cali said to him.

"It's the nature of the beast," he said with a frown.

Against Sam's and his own better judgement, when things were finished in Barrow, King wasn't finished with Cali. She had actually declined his invitation for a vacation together at first. Her brain told her what she should've listened to: not to get further involved with a man who was married to his country. But King had caught her at the perfect moment. She was already tired of Alaska, but couple that with being entangled in something so dangerous that it instantly showed you how fragile life could be, and it gave her a reason to want to live it up, and King was ecstatic that she had. Because for once, he had the same mentality.

He had no idea what would happen next, but for the first time in a while, he had found someone special who knew who he was and what he did, and didn't care. Cali just wanted to be with him, and he just wanted to be with her. She leaned over and gave him a long tequila kiss. The scent of Hawaiian Tropic tanning oil came with it. With the weather, the drinks, and the company, King had become blissfully intoxicated. As for Sam, as she had often done over the years, because she was the adult in their partnership, she waded over with a total buzzkill.

"Sorry to interrupt you two, but duty calls," Sam said.

King finished his kiss. "You're leaving now?"

"Yes, but I managed you two more days here. But that's all Director Lucas was willing to spare."

Cali was happy to hear they had more time together. Her smile sparkled along with the green maze running through her hazel eyes.

"Thanks, Sam. You going to Langley to prepare for our next assignment, I'm assuming?"

"You mean the thankless job that no one else wants or can do?" Sam said. "Yes, that's where I'm going."

"Lucas tell you what it is?"

"Briefly, but don't concern yourself now. Just be ready when I call."

King stepped forward and wrapped Sam in a hug.

Sam pulled away and looked at Cali. "Keep him out of trouble, will you?"

Cali pulled him close. "You mean the thankless job that no one else wants or can do?"

Sam smiled. "Yes, that one." Then to King. She pointed her finger back and forth between him and Cali. "Maybe don't mess this one up?"

That was Sam's way of giving him her stamp of approval. King thought pigs might fly next. Sam waded her way out of the pool, then disappeared into the hotel.

Cali turned toward him and held him at the small of his back. "If you need to go, I'll manage here by myself."

The shot of tequila was hitting him in all the right ways. So was Cali. He knew he didn't have much longer with her, but he planned on making the most of every single second. He knew whatever assignment was next would be another deep dive into the dark side of life. So for now, he planned on soaking up every bit of light he could.

And the bright one standing right in front of him, for the moment, was absolutely all the light he needed.

MOST WANTED

by

Bradley Wright

Book 3 in the Alexander King series.

PRE-ORDER TODAY!

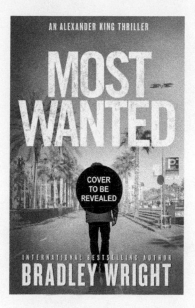

MOST WANTED

by

Bradley Wright

Book 3 in the Alexander King series.
Coming Early 2021

ACKNOWLEDGMENTS

First and foremost, I want to thank you, the reader. I love what I do, and no matter how many people help me along the way, none of it would be possible if you weren't turning the pages.

To my family and friends. Thank you for always being there with mountains of support. You all make it easy to dream, and those dreams are what make it into these books. Without you, no fun would be had, much less novels be written.

To my advanced reader team. You continue to help make everything I do better. You all have become friends, and I thank you for catching those last few sneaky typos, and always letting me know when something isn't good enough. Alexander appreciates you, and so do I.

About the Author

Bradley Wright is the international bestselling author of action-thrillers. The Secret Weapon is his tenth novel. Bradley lives with his family in Lexington, Kentucky. He has always been a fan of great stories, whether it be a song, a movie, a novel, or a binge-worthy television series. Bradley loves interacting with readers on Facebook, Twitter, and via email.

Join the online family:
www.bradleywrightauthor.com
info@bradleywrightauthor.com